PROTECTING My COMMITMENT

SULFUR SPRINGS BOOK 1

TAYLOR RYLAN

Copyright © 2018 by Taylor Rylan

Published in the United States by Taylor Rylan

Cover Design by Jay Aheer of Simply Defined Art

Cover Image by Paul Henry Serres

Proofreading by Sandra Dee of One Love Editing

Copyrights and Trademarks

Alexa

Stetson

*NSYNC

Backstreet Boys

Lucky Charms

Kimber 1911 TLE II

Jeep

Xanax

FBI

Baby One More Time Britney Spears

Collin — 1

The sun glaring in my eyes told me I forgot to close the blinds, again. I really needed to get curtains or something, but I didn't know how much longer I was going to be here. My landlord was a huge asshole and still hadn't returned my calls about renewing my lease.

Remembering Isaac and Jacob's wedding yesterday, the resulting night, and the sexy-as-sin man that had fucked me until we both collapsed just a couple hours ago, I rolled over, hoping to wake him up with a blow job before we both had to get ready for work. But when I rolled over, the bed was empty. I reached for the side of the bed I was sure he'd slept in, but it was cold. Much like the bedroom.

I didn't want any trace of that asshole left, and that meant washing the sheets and then a long, hot shower before I went to Knotty Springs and dealt with another asshole. Since he'd left, I got up and bitched to absolutely nobody as I yanked the covers off the bed. "Dammit! Not again. Fuck! Why does this always happen to me? If they're not trying to hide me, they use me for a night, and then they're gone. Did he think if he stuck around I'd try and marry him or something? What makes him think he's so special anyway? It's not like he was that good-looking or anything. Shit, he's not even the best I've ever had."

"Umm, is there a reason you're destroying the bed?" the deep, rumbly voice from last night asked from the doorway. I slowly turned and there he was. Just as sexy and naked as I remembered. I'd had one drink, and it shouldn't have had any impact on me, but I swear it felt like I was still drunk. "Hey, you okay?"

"Yeah," I croaked out before I dropped the blanket I'd just been yanking on.

"So I just heard you, uh, talking to yourself. You thought I'd left, huh?"

"Yeah." What was I? A parrot?

The man that had done wonderful things to my body last night took a deep breath and looked up before exhaling and looking right back at me. His eyes were just as blue as mine, which was a bit unexpected with how dark his hair was.

"I'm Dalton by the way. I don't think we really got to that yet. I was helping myself to your coffee maker and was coming back to ask you how you took yours. I saw the creamer in the fridge but didn't know if you liked it with a little or a lot."

"A lot. I insult my coffee with too much creamer. I'm sorry. I just…"

"Yeah, you thought I'd fucked you and left. Got it. I should probably go anyway. I have to get home before my shift," Dalton told me as he grabbed his clothes off the floor and quickly pulled them on.

"Wait. Do you want breakfast or coffee? I'm really sorry. I just haven't had the best luck with guys. They're always gone, and you weren't here when I woke up."

"Don't worry about it. I get it," Dalton threw over his shoulder as he left my bedroom. Dammit, this wasn't going well.

"No, wait. I'm really sorry. I mean it. Can I make it up to you? Please? I'd like to explain. I promise I'm not an asshole. You can ask anyone."

"I don't think so. It's probably best if we either forget this happened or just consider it a one and done."

"What? No. Neither," I said as I followed Dalton to the front door. The sun had just risen, but it was stupid cold out, and I was still naked.

"Go inside, Collin. Don't make me arrest you for indecent exposure. You can buy me a coffee later next week. I'm off on Tuesday."

What the fuck? How did he know my name? Like he said, we didn't get that far last night. And I had to wait until Tuesday to see him again? How? I didn't have his number.

I slowly closed the door and went back to the bedroom and finished stripping the bed. After stuffing the sheets and the blanket into the washing machine, and adding probably too much detergent, I hit Start and made my way to the kitchen. Just as he'd said, my coffee maker had a full carafe of freshly brewed coffee. Damn, I was an asshole. I headed to the shower, now regretting I'd have to wash off the smell of the sexy blue-eyed man so soon.

I moaned when I stepped under the steaming hot spray, but it could only do so much for my current mood. I quickly washed and got out to get ready for my day. The project I was currently on was so much more difficult than it had to be. I understood Denver's reasoning, to a certain extent, but the man was making things almost impossible. If Denver wasn't complaining about the project, he was on the phone with his girlfriend. Those were conversations I didn't need to hear. I simply did not understand that man one bit.

I pulled on my khaki cargos and tucked in my shirt before buttoning and zipping my pants. After tugging on thick socks and my boots, I grabbed my wallet, keys, and knife and then went to the kitchen for some much-needed coffee. After checking on the washer and seeing it had just over ten minutes until it was finished, I decided to wait it out so I could throw the bedding in the dryer before leaving for work.

My phone rang as I was pouring my first cup of coffee and dropping bread into the toaster. I looked at the display and it was Sean, one of the two brothers I worked for as a lead architect.

"Hey, Sean. What are you doing up so early?"

"It's not by choice, trust me. And really, eight isn't that early. But I got a call from Denver wondering where you were."

"Dude, it's Sunday. He should be thankful I'm coming over at all. You know how hard it is to find a crew that will work Sundays. As it is, I only convinced half to do it."

"I know. He was pretty pissed you weren't there already. I reminded him it was Sunday, and that it wasn't in our contract to work on Sundays at all."

"That's it. I'm so over that asshole. Why is it I'm always stuck working with assholes all the time?"

"Hey!" Sean mock-yelled before laughing.

"You know I'm not referring to you and Jasper. I'm waiting for my washer so I can throw my sheets in the dryer, and then I'll be on my way. But I'm pulling the guys off of Sundays. We're going back to six days a week. If he's got a problem with it, he can break the contract and find someone else."

"Why do I have a feeling there's more to this than it sounds like."

"Not really, no. He's just always there, complaining. There's something else going on with him, and I haven't figured it out yet.

But he'll get a call or text, and he's gone for a while and then he'll be back. He always has the same question though. When will the project be finished? I keep reminding him that we're not scheduled to be finished until spring. He gets pissed and storms off and then is back about an hour later."

"How long has that been going on?"

"On and off since we started. It wasn't as bad at first. He'd ask maybe once or twice a week. Now it's almost every day. I'd hoped that by adding a Sunday crew, we'd get finished earlier, but it's just not going to happen."

"All right. Jasper and I will have a talk with him. It shouldn't have to come from us. That's something else we're going to resolve, soon. Come to dinner sometime this week so we can discuss some things with you."

"Am I in trouble for any reason, Sean?"

"No, not at all. Jasper and I just have some things we want to run by you, that's all."

"Okay. I'm free all week, so just let me know what your schedules look like and I'll be there. Whose place? Yours or Jasper's?"

"I know Jasper's is closer for you, so I'll see if there works."

"Okay, sounds good," I replied as the washing machine chimed that the cycle was over. I pushed the button on the toaster and dropped the bread and hoped I'd get to eat it while it was still warm.

"You'll hear from me later. Don't work too long today. It's Sunday and we all need a day off. Especially after the party last night."

"Not planning on it. And I left early, so I'm good."

"Okay. Enjoy your day, and you'll hear from me. Bye, Collin."

"Later, Sean." I sat my phone down on the counter and grabbed the butter, a plate, and knife just as my toast popped up. After devouring the buttery goodness and refilling my coffee, I threw my bedding in the dryer and then put on my coat, grabbed my bag and travel mug of coffee, and went out to deal with Denver. Yep, that was just my lot in life it seemed. I needed a vacation.

After arriving at Knotty Springs twenty minutes later, I was greeted by the thunderous glare of Denver Knotts. It was going to be one of those days. It started out like shit, it was obviously going to continue in a downward spiral.

"I'm not in the mood, Denver. So if you're here to bitch about the project not being finished yet, just back the fuck off. I'm in a pissy mood, and I'm not willing to deal with your shit today."

"That's really not how you should be talking to a client, is it? I mean, after all, what if I leave a bad review for your bosses?"

I'd had enough already and I'd only been here for a minute. I grabbed my phone and dialed Sean's number. He picked up immediately.

"Already?"

"I haven't even been here a minute yet. I told him I'm not in the mood to deal with his shit today, and he threatened to leave a bad review for the firm because of how I'm treating him."

"Hand him the phone," Sean growled in my ear. I smiled sweetly and handed Denver—who just glared at me—the phone. I could hear Sean's calm voice through the phone, but as he continued to talk, Denver's face slowly turned a deeper shade of red. It was amazing that it could change so much. I thought maybe it was because he was blond, but nope, I was a blond too, and I couldn't remember my face ever turning that shade.

Denver shot daggers at me and tossed my phone back at me while muttering under his breath before he turned and stormed off.

"Well, he's even more pissed now."

"As he should be. When is your crew set to arrive?"

"Not until ten. It's Sunday. Most of them are giving up time away from their families. I didn't want to ask them to arrive too early."

"All right, call them and tell them no more Sundays. Period. I talked to Jasper. You're coming to dinner at his place tonight, okay?"

"Yeah, sure. What time?"

"Does six work?"

"Yeah, that's fine. I'll see you then. What do you want me to bring? I'm going to send out a group text to my crew and then go do some grocery shopping. I was beginning to wonder when I'd fit it in, so not working today fixes that."

"Just bring yourself. We've got everything planned already."

"Really? I just talked to you not even an hour ago."

"What can I say? I'm fast at planning things. See you tonight, Collin. And enjoy the day off."

I didn't get to say bye before Sean disconnected the call, and Denver was nowhere to be found, so I climbed back in my truck and turned it back on so the heat would warm my fingers and ears. It was early November, but it was already cold. After sending out a group text to my Sunday crew, I buckled my seat belt and put the truck in gear so I could head back to Jackson and the grocery store.

By the time I pulled into the parking lot of the store, I had replies from all of my guys, and they were all okay with the change and were looking forward to a day off. I knew I was. I needed some time to think about everything that'd happened last night and what I needed to do to change things. I knew one thing was for sure: I was finished with men for a while. After what Carter did to me in Alabama…no, after what I allowed Carter to do to me. Because I'd allowed it. For well over a year. Never again. But after that mess, I'd sworn off men, and look at what happened when I let myself be drawn in by pretty blue eyes and dark, brooding looks. I sighed because I really liked those blue eyes and his dark looks. Disgusted with myself, I got out and made my way inside to get my groceries.

After spending close to an hour gathering everything I'd need for the next couple of weeks, I loaded up my purchases into the back seat of my truck and then made my way home to my condo. I hated contacting the owner again about the lease, but I had less than a month left on the current lease, so I needed to know what was what. Unfortunately, my shitty mood got even worse when I arrived back home. There, taped to the door was a note from the landlord. He wasn't willing to renew my lease because of personal reasons. Personal reasons my ass. Just great. I had just under a month to find a new place and move. I just couldn't win today.

After putting away the groceries, I almost grabbed a beer since it was the perfect day to get drunk but thought better of it. I needed to be sober enough to drive later, and that meant no drinking. Unfortunately. So I sorted the rest of my laundry and started it while listening to Alexa play my cleaning playlist. I started sorting and organizing my townhouse now that I'd have to move soon, and I knew there was stuff I didn't want to take with me.

Three bags of trash later, I realized I'd missed lunch, so I threw together a quick sandwich. I'd be eating dinner with Sean,

Jasper, Simon, and Liam soon enough. Maybe they'd have some ideas of a place to rent. What I really needed to do was find somewhere to buy. But was I ready to make that commitment? Was I ready to be a homeowner? Was I even going to stay in Wyoming? I guess I needed to figure that out before I thought about making a commitment like that.

Deciding to stop at the home improvement store for some boxes after going to Jasper and Liam's, I changed out of my dusty clothes before I once again grabbed my coat and everything else I needed to leave.

Boxes and tape were cheaper there than at the discount store, and they had more of them anyway, so I headed out to have dinner and prepare to start the process of moving. Again. The end of the month was going to be here before I knew it.

Dalton — 2

Shit. What was I thinking? I'd had one drink last night. One. That's it. I knew better than to hook up with someone that in some way would know my boss. And anyone at Jacob and Isaac's wedding somehow knew them. So what did I do? I let my dick talk and hit on the sexy blond I saw sitting with a set of identical twins. They were gorgeous, but I knew they were both married and therefore off-limits. But the blond who looked like he belonged in a boy band, he wasn't wearing a ring, and I noticed he didn't seem to have a date with him, so I took a chance and worked my charm. It worked and before I knew it, we were at his place and I was buried deep in him.

I lost track of how many condoms we went through, but I remember it being several. I'd really hoped to have a turn on the receiving end this morning, but I'd already been standing there when he started mumbling to himself, thinking I'd snuck out in the night. I'll admit, I'd had more than my fair share of one-night stands before, but that's not where I was in my life anymore. That's not what I was looking for. I was too damn old for that shit.

I knew I'd been lumped in with the previous assholes in Collin's life, so I'd decided to split. Plus, I'd been confused by him being mad thinking I'd left, but he'd even said he didn't think I was that special anyway, so why stick around? I definitely could have seen myself taking him to dinner if he'd let me. But not if he saw me as a one and done. So maybe having coffee with Collin wasn't the best thing. No matter how I looked at it, he thought I'd skipped out and ranted about me. He didn't know me from Adam, so to talk about me like that was harsh, but I wonder what caused him to be so distrusting?

I didn't have his number, not that I couldn't easily get it, but the more I thought about it, the more I was convinced it wasn't a good idea. Now, worried that things were going to be awkward the next time I saw him, I hoped like hell I didn't run into him in Crooked Bend. I should have thought about that before I went home with him. Although, his place was in Jackson, and I lived in Sulfur Springs, so chances of us actually running into each other seemed in my favor.

"Andrews!"

"What?" I snapped back at Seth. We were on our own for the next week or so while Jacob was off on his honeymoon with his new hubby. They were lucky they'd found each other. I hadn't yet found a guy that could get me to say *I do*. I wasn't against it, but it seemed more and more men were already taken, or they didn't want the same things, or like this morning, they had more issues than I could deal with.

"If you're going to be an even crankier asshole than you normally are, I'm taking vacation."

"You're the one that yelled at me."

"Only because I've said your name half a dozen times. You're the one who was sitting there like you'd eaten bad Chinese for breakfast."

"I didn't get much sleep last night. What did you want?"

"How did you not get much sleep? You left almost as early as the grooms."

"None of your business. Now, did you actually want something, or did you just want to annoy me?"

"I actually wanted something. Did you ever hear back from Lieutenant Rivers over in Sulfur Springs?"

"No, last I heard, they were calling in some big-shot investigator or something. He said they'd get back to us if they needed to. Why?"

"I wanted to close out the report, but I needed to know if they had any more information. I mean, come on, it's slow around here on a good day."

"Well, I guess give him a call and see if he has any news for you. You can't close out the report until the case is closed though.

Just archive it and it'll leave your open-case files, and you won't have to look at it every time you open your computer."

"Oh, thanks. How did you know that? You're newer than me."

"Yeah, but I've been around longer. I may have only been with Wildlife Services for five years, but I'd spent over a decade with the Denver PD before that."

"You don't have to rub it in, Andrews."

"I'm not, Jeffries. Why are you bugging me? Shouldn't you be mooning over Jill or something? Wait, where's Jill?"

"It's Sunday. She's off today. Unfortunately for me, I'm off tomorrow, so we won't get to spend time together until next weekend."

"Says who? Finish your report and go bug your girlfriend. There's nothing going on. And Cruz covers the evening shift by himself all the time."

"Yeah, but there's even less going on then."

"Look, I just told you to go home and snuggle with your girl. If you don't, then that's on you."

I got up and went to the coffeepot and poured myself another mug. It was going to be an incredibly long and boring day, and I had nobody to blame but myself for the reason for my crabbiness.

"I don't have to be told twice. I'll see you either tomorrow or Tuesday."

"I'm off Tuesday, so you'll see me tomorrow or Wednesday. Either works for me. Enjoy some time with Jill," I said as I sat down and pulled up the paperwork I'd told Jacob I'd file while he was on his honeymoon. I needed to keep busy, and the best way to do that was to bury myself in work. There was decidedly less busywork in Crooked Bend, but there was no way I was going back to Denver PD. I'd left because there were too many dirty cops, and I was tired of the system looking the other way.

Wildlife Services was more than welcoming, but I ended up working alone more than I realized I would. Because of my position in the Denver PD, at the time, I didn't want anyone in my personal life. I never knew if I'd come home or not, and that wasn't something I wanted to put a partner through. But that didn't mean I wanted to be completely isolated either. When I started with Wildlife Services, I dated a couple of men, but nothing serious came of it. They were just looking for a good fuck, and that's about it. I didn't like the long hours working alone, so when Jacob had an opening, I'd jumped at the chance to apply. I was ready for a change in scenery, even if it wasn't much of a difference between Cheyenne and Sulfur Springs.

But I had plenty of room for Knight, and we spent more time together than ever. I needed that time with my horse. He'd gotten me through a lot of shit over the past few years. I'd thought about getting another horse, but I didn't have as much time as I needed to commit to two, so poor Knight was the only horse in the stable.

My place was on the small size for Wyoming, only around fifty acres that I had no intention of adding anything else to, except maybe another horse one day. And possibly a dog. I missed my old dog Bandit, but he'd been gone for years. I left home shortly after he'd passed and hadn't had time for one since. I made time for Knight, so I could probably make time for a dog as well. Especially now that I wasn't going anywhere. I'd finally broken down and bought a place; it was time to stay put.

"Hey, man. Where's Seth?"

I looked up at Gavin and thought again that he reminded me of someone, but I couldn't quite put my finger on who.

"I sent him home earlier. He was moaning about how Jill was off today and he wasn't. He's off tomorrow, and they wouldn't get to spend time together until next week."

"Wow. Where were you when you told him to go home?"

"What do you mean? I was sitting right here. I got tired of listening to him gripe. Why?"

"You realize they live together, right?"

"What? Since when?"

"I don't know. Maybe a week ago? They're 'in love' and things seem to be moving pretty quick with them."

"So he got a free day off, didn't he?"

"Yep, because he'd see her all evening, and I'd imagine all night."

"When's your next evening off?"

"Friday. Why?"

"You work Saturday?"

"Yeah. And Sunday."

"Well, now you've got Saturday off, too. I'm texting the little jerk now."

Gavin laughed at me as I fired off a text to Seth. I wasn't playing those games. I really needed to stop thinking about a certain blond so I could focus on shit at work.

Me: Congratulations! Your sad story that I fell for just landed you Saturday evening's shift. So not only are you covering Friday evening, but Saturday as well. I chuckled as I watched the bubbles appear, letting me know that Seth was replying. There was no way he wasn't going to be pissed.

Seth: What are you talking about? I'm already working Friday evening.

Me: I'm aware of that. Now you're working Saturday as well.

Seth: Why? You said I could go home.

Me: Yeah, but only because you made it sound like you wouldn't get to spend any time with Jill. You failed to mention to me that you two moved in together a week ago.

Seth: What's that got to do with anything?

Me: Really? You won't get to see her because you had to work today and she didn't? Really? YOU LIVE WITH HER. You're now working on Saturday evening, so make sure you tell your 'roomie' why.

Seth: You're an asshole.

Me: That's not news. Deal with the consequences.

I tossed my phone on the desk and ignored the buzzing as Seth kept bombarding me with messages. When he realized I wasn't going to respond, he called, but thankfully Gavin picked up the phone. I heard him laugh in the background, but I tuned the call out and went back to filing the reports. An hour later, I was at a good stopping point and was more than ready to head home, so I saved everything and logged off the computer.

"Have a good evening, Dalton," Gavin said as I pulled on my coat.

"Yeah, you too. I don't know how you do it every evening, but I'm thankful you do."

"You know I spend a lot of time reading. Jacob doesn't mind, and it's not like I'm required to do a ton of patrols. Just once or twice. It's an easy enough job. Although, it does get boring."

"Yeah, I know. We're supposed to get another deputy, but I'm not sure when."

"Whenever works for me. Some evenings a couple guys from the police station will come down and hang out. It helps pass the time."

"That's understandable. Well, don't do anything I wouldn't do," I said as I walked out the door and into the bitter cold. The sun was almost gone, and it was only just after five. That combined with the winds made for a miserable night. I needed to get home so I could check in on Knight and make sure he was okay, but he'd lived in harsher climates, so I was sure he was fine.

Twenty minutes later, after pulling my cruiser into the garage beside my seldom-used truck, I plugged the block heater in before I went inside to quickly change out of my uniform. I needed to make sure I gave my boy an extra bit of love since I was late this morning and rushed through the morning routine with him.

After changing into old jeans and a flannel shirt and pulling on my work boots, I grabbed an apple from the refrigerator and headed to the stable. It was big enough for four other horses, and I'd always kept all of the stalls clean and ready to go, which came in handy this morning. I needed to clean two stalls tonight—the price I had to pay for spending last night with the sexy blond with the wicked smile.

Knight greeted me when I opened the door to the stables, and I smiled. At least he was always happy to see me.

"Hey, boy. How are you doing? You ready for a little bit of outside time? I have to clean up in here, so why don't you go out and play in the snow for a bit?" I was talking to my horse, but I didn't care. I pulled his turnout coat off the hook it was hanging on, and he whinnied again, knowing what it meant.

"Yeah, yeah. You're going outside. But only for a bit. I'll give you more time outside tomorrow." I tossed the coat over his broad back and then secured it before opening the door that led to the corral. Knight moseyed out the door and pranced around like the king of the yard that he was. Damn horse. I just shook my head and set about mucking out the stalls.

By the time I had both clean and one ready for my boy for the night, I opened the door and was greeted by my baby's dark head. "You want your dinner, huh?" I asked him as I took off the coat and then let him into his bed for the night. He immediately went to the feed bucket, looking for his grain, and came out with the apple I'd hidden in there.

I grabbed the curry comb and started grooming him, and by the time I'd made it to his feet and checked his hooves, he was finished with his supper and was just standing there, patiently waiting for me to finish his grooming session.

"All right, boy. It's time for me to go find my own meal. I promise you'll get more outside time tomorrow." I gave Knight's velvety-soft nose another rub before I left his stall and latched the door. It was definitely time to find something for my own supper, and I seriously needed to think about getting a dog. Evenings were too quiet without one, and I wasn't good company for myself. There were a couple of cats that came and went, but they lived out there. I needed a dog. Maybe. But what I really wanted was the sexy blue-eyed blond that made me feel something last night. It was too bad he obviously had too many issues.

Collin — 3

"What's wrong?"

"Huh? Oh, what makes you think something's wrong?" I asked Jasper, who was giving me a knowing smile.

"Maybe because you're not eating and the rest of us started a few minutes ago?" Sean chimed in. I looked down, and sure enough, everyone else had started in on their pizza while mine was still untouched. Shit. What was wrong with me? No, I knew what my problem was. And he had dark hair, sexy tattoos, and bright blue eyes.

"You want to tell us what's going on? Or are we going to have to guess?" Jasper asked. I was torn between confessing and keeping quiet, but Sean and Jasper had become great friends since I'd started working for them. Hell, I'd even stayed with Jasper and Liam when I first got here.

"I've got a lot of my mind right now. I honestly don't know where to start."

"How about with you and Dalton?" Sean asked. I know my eyes got huge. How did he know about that? I'd just met him last night.

"Everyone saw you two leave the wedding reception shortly after the grooms did," Sean told me.

Well, shit. I sometimes forgot that in small towns, everyone knew everything. Thankfully, I lived in Jackson, and it was a little bigger and easier to hide.

"Just because we left at the same time doesn't mean we left together. I'll have you know, I drove home in my own vehicle last night."

"Really? You're telling me you didn't have Jacob's sexy deputy follow you? Although, the one that works evenings is hot, too. But I swear, he's as straight as they come," Liam told us.

"You're just asking for another spanking, aren't you?" Jasper asked his husband with a not-so-friendly look on his face. I didn't blame him for being a little possessive of his husband. Liam was cute, but really not my type. So Dalton was one of Jacob's deputies? Now I knew where I could find him to ask him for coffee, I guess. His comment about arresting me for indecent exposure sure made more sense now.

"Off topic," Sean said, so everyone looked back at me from watching Liam and Jasper.

"Anyway. Do you know anything at all about what Denver's deal is?" I asked, hoping to change the subject.

"I've thought about it today and think our best bet might be to ask Hawke. He's his brother, so I'd hope he'd know what's going on with Denver. If nothing else, it never hurts to ask."

"I'll swing by the bakery tomorrow and talk to him; I'm pretty sure he's working, and I'm due for some coffee cake anyway. I mean, he might know something, right?"

"Okay. Anything else bothering you? I know you sounded quite upset this morning, and it was only just after eight."

"Just a lot going on. My landlord decided, for personal reasons, to not renew my lease. So I have a little over three weeks to find somewhere and move. That's really weighing on me."

"I wish I could say I'm surprised, but I'm not. You've had nothing but issues with him since right after you moved in," Sean said. I had to agree though. My landlord wasn't the greatest at anything except making my life hell.

"I know. So if you know of anywhere for rent, I'd appreciate it if you sent the info my way."

"We can do that. But we really don't have a whole lot of knowledge about rentals over in Jackson anymore," Jasper told me. I realized that they all lived in Crooked Bend basically.

"Yeah, it doesn't have to be in Jackson. At this point, I'll take just about anywhere as long as it's safe and the roof doesn't leak."

"We'll ask around, but I know Jacob's house is empty. He was thinking about selling it though. Maybe he'd be willing to rent it to you for a while. Although, he's in Hawaii on his honeymoon, so you'll have to wait until he gets back next week," Simon told me. That could certainly work. I wouldn't imagine that Jacob would be a terrible landlord.

"Yeah, that could certainly work. I'll ask him next week. In the meantime, I'll start looking over in Jackson. I just didn't need that dropped on me today after everything with Denver."

"Speaking of work, there's something Jasper and I wanted to talk to you about."

"Have I done something wrong?"

"No, not at all. Sean and I have been talking, and we think you've done an amazing job. We've really appreciated all you've done for us and the company, and we realize you're already a lead architect with the firm, but we'd like to offer you the position of full partner as well. We know it's a huge decision, and we don't expect an answer tonight or anything."

"Wow" was all I could get out. They couldn't be serious, could they? They'd worked really hard to make their business as successful as it was. "I really don't know what to say. I'm incredibly honored. If you'd let me think about it for a day or two, I'd appreciate it."

"Take all the time you need. The offer is open. You've been a huge asset, Collin. And without all of the hard work you've put in, we wouldn't be nearly as far as we are," Sean told me. I was still a little shocked and basically flabbergasted.

I couldn't really recover from the bombshell they'd dropped on me, and I was so excited as well as nervous, I didn't eat. I picked at my pizza, something I rarely did.

"We should have waited until after he'd eaten," Jasper said to the rest of the room. He had an apologetic look on his face, which made me feel bad.

"Naw, it's okay. I really just have a lot on my mind right now."

"I know it's not ideal, but you're more than welcome to come room with us again. The room you stayed in is just as you left it. It might be a little dustier, and I know Liam has added some things to the closet, but if you need a place to stay, you're welcome here."

When I had first come to work for their company, Jasper had let me live with them while I adjusted to the area and found a place to stay. "Thanks, Jasper. I really do appreciate that. If I can't find anything, I might have to take you up on that. Right now, I think I'll head on out and swing by and pick up some boxes. I should probably start packing up the things I don't really need on a regular basis."

"Oh, don't go yet. I picked up a cake earlier if you want to stay. I know you haven't really eaten though," Liam told me. I felt bad, but really, I just wanted to go home.

"I appreciate it. But I really just want to go home and try to make heads or tails of things. I'll let you two know what I decide about the partnership," I told Jasper and Sean as I got up from the table.

"Here, at least take some pizza home. You may not be hungry now, but you might be later after you spend some time packing," Liam said as he hurriedly placed several slices of pizza in a bag for me to take home with me.

"Thanks, Liam. I really appreciate it."

"No thanks needed. Do you want some cake, too?"

"Nope. I'm good. But thanks," I said before smiling at the feisty blond and then giving him a quick hug. I quickly said goodbye to the rest of the guys, and then I was on my way to the home improvement store to pick up some boxes for packing. It wasn't really something I was looking forward to doing, but I wasn't going to be able to get around it.

After parking in the oversized lot at the store, I rushed in out of the cold and grabbed a cart. I needed packing supplies, and lots of them, so a cart was the way to go. Once I'd procured and paid for my purchases, I loaded them up in the back seat of my truck and headed home. The sooner I had things ready to go, the better

I'd feel about the entire situation. Three weeks wasn't nearly enough time to do all I had to do. Especially not with time off between Christmas and New Year's next month rapidly approaching.

When I pulled into my covered parking space at my townhouse, I groaned at the thought of packing up and moving everything. Making several trips, I hauled the boxes, tape, and other supplies into my place and set them down in the living room.

I needed to think about more than just moving though. Jasper and Sean had made me a very generous offer, one I'd be incredibly crazy to turn down. If I was even considering accepting, and let's be honest, I was, then maybe it was time to buy a place instead of renting. Maybe it was time to put down roots. But, thinking that, I knew I really needed to talk to my brother. He'd been asking me for years when I was coming back to California. Not knowing exactly where he was, or even if he was in the country right now or not, I sent a text to see if it'd be possible to talk. I smiled when my phone immediately rang. I plopped down on the couch and got comfortable before I answered. If tonight was anything like our past phone calls, I'd be talking to my brother for quite some time.

"Hey, Daniel. How's it going?"

"It's going. What are you up to? You finally coming home yet?"

I laughed nervously, which gave me away.

"You're not coming home, are you?"

"I've been offered a partner position. I'm seriously considering it. It's a great opportunity, and it really couldn't have come at better time. I'm going to be moving again, and now I'm thinking maybe I should look for somewhere to buy instead of somewhere to rent. Daniel? Are you still there?"

"Yeah. I'm just processing. Why are you moving? I thought you were happy where you were?"

"Happy here in Jackson, yes. But my landlord has been pure hell since I moved in."

"What? Why didn't you say anything?"

"There was nothing to say, really. Just normal asshole behavior."

"When are you moving?"

"By the end of the month. I'm going to have to move into a temporary place for a bit first. I can't close on a house in three weeks, but I might have a place I can rent. The sheriff in Crooked Bend just got married, and his place is empty. But he's on his honeymoon right now, so I can't exactly see if he's willing to rent his house to me."

"Wow. Wasn't that the wedding you were at last night?"

"Yeah. How did you know that? Until you called, I wasn't even sure if you were out on assignment or not."

"Not on assignment. I'm taking some time off."

"Really? Everything okay?"

"You're not going to change the subject, Collin. But everything's fine. I'm just getting a little restless and wanted some time off. You know I love my job, but there's only so many assignments I can handle before I want time off. Now, you going to tell me about the wedding or not?"

"Well, since I know for a fact that I didn't tell you about the wedding, or when I was going, you tell me how the wedding went. Are you here, or is someone else spying on me?"

"Nope, not there. But I heard James talking about the wedding to Taylor. I guess they let the grooms borrow their plane for the flight to Hawaii for their honeymoon. So, you want to tell me what you're hiding?"

"Nothing. I'm just…Daniel, you ever wonder about why things happen? Why so many things that could all be good, all seem to happen at once? Is it a sign?"

"Maybe. What are you referring to though?"

"I was just thinking that maybe I'm supposed to be here? That maybe Wyoming is meant to be my home."

"How so? Because you were offered a partner position?"

"Not just that. On top of that, I have to move, so maybe it's time to buy a place and settle down. I mean, think about it. Out of the eight of us, how many of us are actually settled?"

"Well, Brian's married; so is Andrew."

"Yeah, and that's it."

"You thinking about getting married? I didn't even know you were seeing anyone."

"I'm hoping to start seeing someone. Maybe. I'm not sure. It's new. Very, very new and I'm not sure where we stand yet."

"Okay, maybe you should back up and start from the beginning."

Dalton — 4

It was my day off, and it wasn't starting out the greatest. I woke up to realize I was out of coffee. How did that happen? Actually, I knew how it happened. I couldn't stop thinking about a certain blond-haired, blue-eyed man I'd spent Saturday night with. I knew where he lived, but I hadn't given him anything other than my name. Although, Dalton was unique enough that he could track me down if he wanted.

But before I could even contemplate hunting Collin down, I needed coffee. It was rough taking care of Knight before I'd had a cup of coffee, but I did it. Since I knew I was a grouchy asshole without my morning coffee, I parked in front of Son of a Biscuit to get my morning brew before I braved the store to get more coffee beans. I was met with the heavenly aroma of coffee and baked goods as I entered the bakery, and already I was starting to feel better.

"Hey, Deputy Andrews. You not working today?" Angie, the girl behind the counter, asked as I walked up.

"No, it's my day off, and I'm out of coffee at home. Please tell me you have coffee."

She giggled when I winked at her. She was entirely too young for me, and she had the wrong parts, but I'd found that a little flirting could get you places you normally wouldn't get.

"Of course we have coffee. And it's Tuesday. Which means that Rhett is working, and that means there are pumpkin scones. They're all gone right now, but I know he has more in the oven."

Rhett was the owner of the bakery, and his pumpkin scones were to die for. I snatched them up whenever I could. But any other time, it was coffee cake. One of the bakers had this apple cinnamon coffee cake that was bliss.

"Okay, I'll take a few of those when they're done, and while I wait for pumpkin scones, got any coffee cake? And of course, the largest coffee you have."

"Sure thing. If you take a seat, I'll bring everything to you when it's ready. How much coffee cake do you want? Your usual?"

"Yes, please." I smiled as I handed over my credit card. Once I signed the receipt and put my card back in my wallet, I found an open table for two and relaxed.

I was lost in thought when Angie brought out my coffee. "Here you go, Deputy Andrews. I'm waiting on the coffee cake, too. Sorry. I didn't realize that Collin was in the back. He always snatches Hawke's coffee cake when it comes out of the oven. Like you, he takes the whole loaf. But there's several; I'm just waiting for them to bring it out front."

"Thanks, Angie. I appreciate it." What were the chances that it was the same Collin? It was a common enough name, so maybe not. I couldn't seem to get the man out of my mind, but was he someone I wanted to give a chance? It hurt a bit that he assumed I'd skipped out on him and said all that stuff. Hell, my clothes were still on his bedroom floor if he'd have just looked.

I took a tentative sip of the steaming black brew that I'd quickly found was the best coffee in Crooked Bend, Sulfur Springs, and Jackson. It was only just a quick walk from the station, and I was in here daily, getting a large black coffee.

"Fancy meeting you here. I was told you were the one who was waiting for my coffee cake and some scones," Collin said as he placed both on the table in front of me.

"Your coffee cake?"

"Yeah. Well, not really. I'm in here as often as I can so I can swipe a coffee cake or two from Hawke. I've already eaten one and was hoping for another when Angie said the deputy was out front waiting for his coffee cake. I have to assume that's you? So you're a deputy?"

"Sit down, Collin," I said as I nudged the other chair out. He actually listened and sat across from me. When our knees bumped each other's under the too-small table, he unfortunately moved his chair farther back. It wasn't like I hadn't already touched every part of his body on Saturday night.

"So, a deputy?"

"Yes. I work for Jacob. Which was why I was at his wedding reception. I wasn't going to go at all, but at the last minute I decided why not."

"Is that how you knew my name?"

"No. I looked at the magazine that was on your counter while I was brewing coffee."

"Oh. You going to let me apologize about what happened? I really am sorry. There's a reason for what I did, but that still doesn't make it right."

"There usually is. Fine, apology accepted. Better now?"

"Not really. I feel that you're going to hold it against me."

"No, Collin, I'm not. But I really don't think there's anything else for us to talk about."

When his blue eyes met mine, he couldn't hide the hurt in them. "I deserve that. I understand. Well, I'll leave you to your breakfast. Have a good day, Deputy," Collin said as he got up and hurried back behind the counter and into the kitchen. Obviously he was a close enough friend that he could just come and go in and out of the kitchen.

No longer really interested in sticking around and enjoying my coffee cake, I picked up the box with the cake, the bag with the scones, and my coffee and left. I needed to hit the store and stock up on groceries anyway, so it was time to get my day started. Until we got more deputies, I only had one day off a week. I needed to make the most of it, and I had more than enough to do.

I passed Logan on his way in, and he looked like he always did on Tuesdays, upset that his husband was at the bakery instead of out at the ranch. After climbing into my truck, which I rarely used anymore, I headed over to Jackson so I could hit the superstore and get my household supplies for the next week or two. I never had the same day off two weeks in a row, and with snow already on the ground, we never knew what to expect, other than to be prepared for it all.

After a painful hour at the store, I headed back to my place in hopes of spending some time with Knight. I didn't get to ride him nearly as often as I hoped, but I could certainly spend some time pampering him. And that's what I did. After getting the groceries in the house and put away, I ate half of the coffee cake and one of the scones before heading out to the stable to give my boy the attention he deserved.

By the time I came back in the house, it was afternoon and the goodies I'd eaten were long gone. Not really in the mood to cook, but not wanting to head back to town to get something, I opted for eating a sandwich. I needed a shower before I was fit to be around anyone else, and I was sick of my own company, so after devouring a ham-and-cheese sandwich, I hit the shower and then quickly got dressed. Once I had a plan in place, I headed to the animal rescue over in Jackson. It was time to see if I could find a companion that could stand my company. I'd spent too many years alone.

"Hi, welcome to Second Chance Sanctuary. What can we help you with?" a too-cheerful middle-aged woman asked as soon as I entered the building.

"I was interested in meeting your dogs if I could."

"Sure thing. Are you looking for a lost pet, or are you looking to adopt?"

"Adopt. I'm tired of my own company in the evenings."

"That's understandable. Right this way. We have sixteen dogs right now, and sadly, more on the way. Have a look, and if anyone catches your eye, just let me know, and I'll get you set up in a meet-and-greet room if you'd like."

"Thanks," I told her as I walked down the row of kennels. I didn't want a dog that was too small because I was afraid something would happen to it out at the ranch. Anything midsized and up was a possibility though. But what caught my attention was a high-pitched whine from the end. When I looked at the end kennel, my eyes locked with a pair of sad brown ones.

"Ah, yes. That's Daisy. She's a sweetheart but has a sad story."

"What's her story?" I asked as I walked to her kennel and knelt down. My fingers were quickly kissed when I stuck them between the links in the kennel door.

"That's just it—she was brought in as a stray. No microchip, nothing. We've waited for months for someone to claim her, but nothing. She's a little stubborn but super sweet. She'll need an experienced owner, so if you've never had a dog before, I wouldn't recommend her."

"I've had dogs most of my life until recent years. But I finally have time for another dog. Can I meet her?" I asked, and before I could prepare for it, I found myself full of approximately eighty pounds of a very excited German shepherd named Daisy. I knew I was going to get hell for her name, but I didn't care. I already knew she was absolutely perfect, and I needed her as much as she needed me.

"I can see you've already made your choice. Why don't we go up front and you can fill out the paperwork? You don't live in an apartment, do you?"

"No. I have fifty acres and a blue roan outside of Sulfur Springs. I don't have a fence, but I can put something up if that's required."

"It usually is, but Daisy has never run off. Ever. Which doesn't make any sense at all since she was a stray."

"Do you think that maybe she got left behind by a family on vacation?"

"I'm not sure. She's very well mannered, and the vet's guess is she's only around two years old. She was already fixed, so we assumed that meant she had all of her shots as well."

I filled out the paperwork and couldn't help reaching down and giving her ears a scratch or two. After I handed the paperwork back, the lady who I learned was named Anne smiled and took it to an office. Hopefully, I'd get to take my new friend home. Yeah, I worked long hours, but I was almost positive that Jacob wouldn't have any issues with me bringing Daisy into work with me. He'd brought Ivan in several times. As bosses went, he was one of the best I'd ever worked with.

"Deputy Andrews?"

"Yes?" I looked toward the voice that called for me. I was met by yet another blond, this one younger than Collin but just as good-looking.

"Hi, I'm Xander Garrison. I'm filling in for my boss right now, who happens to also be my mother. She's on a cruise with her new husband. So you're going to be taking our Daisy girl away from us?"

At the mention of her name, Daisy whined and went directly to Xander's side, and he obliged and crouched down beside her and gave her a hug.

"If you're attached to her, I understand and can meet some of the other dogs. But I'll admit, I'm feeling connected to her."

"No. I'm not the right home for Daisy, but she's a sweetheart. I find it a little ironic that a sheriff's deputy is ending up with a German shepherd though. Tell me, will she be going to work with you?"

"Every chance she gets, yes."

"Let's get the rest of the paperwork complete so you two can head home to Sulfur Springs," Xander said as he looked at the application. Looked like I'd just adopted a beautiful lady named Daisy.

Collin — 5

I was pissed when Angie came to the back and told me I couldn't take both of the coffee cakes that had just come out of the oven. Rhett laughed and Hawke giggled at me. I glared and was about to growl at them until Angie said who exactly wanted the coffee cake and some pumpkin scones. I was only too happy to volunteer to take them out to him, hoping it was my deputy.

Too bad he didn't seem any more interested in me than he did when he left Sunday morning. Really, I had nobody to blame but myself. But dammit, I wanted another chance to make it up to him. But in over a week, still nothing from him. He knew where I lived, and all I knew was where he worked.

I was standing outside of the Crooked Bend sheriff's department, but unfortunately, I wasn't here to see Dalton. Sean had said that Jacob and Isaac were back from their honeymoon, and Jacob was back at work if I wanted to swing by and talk about his house. If I happened to see a blue-eyed deputy, well, that was an added perk.

The door chimed as I entered, and I was greeted with a whine before a bark, and then a German shepherd was charging toward me.

"Daisy, no!" the man I'd been dreaming about said, but it was too late. I was on my back with a very excited Daisy licking my face. I couldn't help it; I laughed and gave her a big hug. Daniel loved German shepherds and had two of the most well-behaved ones I'd ever met. Fritz and Optimus were Daniel's babies, and I missed them. Maybe I should seriously consider going back to California for Christmas next month.

"I'm sorry, Collin. Daisy, get off of him," Dalton said as he grabbed Daisy's collar and pulled her off me. I sat up and looked around the station. I'd never been inside before as I'd never had a reason. "Are you stalking me now?" Dalton asked, a little harshly.

"You wish. Trust me, I got the message loud and clear, asshole."

"Collin is here to see me," Jacob said as he reached out to help me up off the floor. "I see you've met Daisy, our unofficial mascot. She seems quite taken with you, although she ignores most everyone else."

"Yeah, well, what can I say? Dogs love me. Sean said you—"

"Yep. Why don't we just head over there now. I can show you the house, and you can let me know what your thoughts are."

"That sounds great. I have to get back to the site we're working at in a bit. The owner is a little high-strung and is making my life hell. But honestly, I really don't want to move back in with Jasper and Liam if I don't have to. I really like Jasper, and his husband is adorable, but those two are loud in the bedroom. And out of it. Usually out of it."

Jacob laughed a deep belly laugh, and I couldn't help but join him. "But seriously, I really appreciate you taking the time to show me the place."

"It's really not a problem at all. Let me grab my coat and keys, and I'll be right with you." I watched as Jacob turned and walked back into his office. I gave Dalton a fleeting glance before nodding and turning to leave. Daisy whined again, but I kept walking. I needed to get out of there as quickly as I could. I opened the door and went to stand in front of my truck. Thankfully, Jacob joined me just a few moments later.

"Sorry about that. Honestly, normally Daisy is very well behaved."

"It's fine. I love dogs; I just haven't been allowed to have one where I live. Maybe when I buy a place."

"Well, Isaac and I have been talking about it, and we will eventually want to sell the place, so if you're interested in buying, just let us know."

"I'm not sure just yet. I have a lot to think about right now, and I'm still trying to figure it all out. You'd think it would be easier since I'm thirty-two, but it's not."

"Don't worry about it. We're more than happy to rent the place to you if you're interested. Come on, I'll show you the house, and then you can let me know if you're my new tenant or not. It's not a far drive, but it's too damn cold to walk, so give me a sec to get into my truck, and I'll lead you over."

"Sounds good," I said before I climbed into the still-warm cab of my truck. When I looked toward the station, I saw both Dalton and Daisy standing in the door. Interesting. I had to put the deputy out of my mind though, because he'd made it clear he wasn't interested.

After driving a few blocks, I pulled in behind Jacob, and I already knew I was interested in the place. Not only was it well kept, it was perfect for me. Jacob's place was set on the edge of town, and it was very well maintained.

"It's nothing like Isaac's cabin, and not nearly as big, but it does have an acre with it if you wanted to get a dog. I have no issues with pets—just let me know if you decide to get one."

"I haven't even considered it before seeing Daisy, honestly. Right now, I'm just hoping to find somewhere to live."

"I can understand that," Jacob said as he unlocked the front door. The place was cute and empty. It was larger than the townhouse I was currently in, and I knew I wouldn't have any issues with fitting my stuff in it. "It has three bedrooms upstairs and a smaller one down here off of the kitchen in the back. I used it as a home office because really, that's about all it's good for. It's too small for much. We did remove all of the furniture but left the kitchen appliances. We really would feel better if the place had someone in it. Although, it's close enough that I can check on it every day, but I have a feeling we're in for a bad winter this year."

"When aren't we in for a bad winter? I've lived here for a little over a year, and last winter was brutal, but Jasper and Sean have told me all about the previous winters. I'm a California boy, and after I left there, I was in Alabama. I've never seen so much snow before."

"Yeah, we tend to get a lot of it. But feel free to look around, and let me know if you have any questions. I'm going to step out onto the back deck and give Isaac a call. He's texted my phone at least half a dozen times since I left the station. I need to make sure everything is okay with Mack."

"Go call your hubby. I won't be long," I said as I turned and went back to the stairs. After spending the better part of ten minutes looking around, I agreed with my first impression. I'd found home. Now I just needed to go let Jacob know. I found him downstairs in the kitchen. He was sitting on the counter waiting for me.

"Sorry to keep you waiting."

"Nope, don't be. I wasn't doing much of anything. Just paperwork I have to get filed with the county. It seems that my life is mostly paperwork. So, what's the verdict?"

"It's a great place. I really like it, and I'd love to take it off your hands. But I know we can't close on a sale in the two-week timeframe my current landlord gave me. Do you think I can rent it while we figure out the sale and stuff?"

"So you're interested in buying it? You're sure?"

"Yeah. It's time to put down roots, and Jasper and Sean offered me a partner position. I haven't accepted or declined, but I know what I want to do now. I'll always miss California, but I just feel that this is where I'm supposed to be."

"We'll get something drawn up for you. How about you go ahead and move in, and then think about it? Any rent you pay me, I'll knock off of the asking price if you decide to buy it. I don't want you to feel you're rushed or anything. Especially since I know you work out of the Jackson office."

"I appreciate it. But I think it's time to find a place to stay put."

"That I can understand. That was one of the reasons why I bought this place. I'll get something drawn up, and you can swing by tomorrow and sign it. I'll give you the keys then. Does that work?"

"Yeah. I'll give my brothers a call and see if they can come and help me move. They've been harping on me to come visit. Well, maybe they should visit me instead," I told Jacob, and he shook his head while smiling.

"I only have Marie, and yeah, she's not the type to help me move."

"Well, she has a bunch of kids, doesn't she?"

"Yeah. Jasmine was their fourth. And according to her, the last. Heath doesn't care how many they have; he just wants my sister to be happy."

I stood on the porch while Jacob locked the front door. This was it. I felt like I was finally putting down roots.

"What time tomorrow works for you?"

"Any, really. I'm working on a project over at Knotty Springs Ranch in Sulfur Springs. I can swing over here whenever you need me to. Denver is driving me crazy, but Sean had a talk with him, and he's backed off some. He's tolerable now, which is a relief."

"Okay. How about eleven thirty? That way, you can swing by the diner and grab lunch before heading back out to no-man's-land. Doesn't he have a bunch of hot springs on his place? I'm trying to remember his area of the county."

"Yeah, he does. Which is the reason for the construction project. He's trying to capitalize on it by having a bunch of spa houses built near the natural pools. It's a great idea, but he wants everything done with natural supplies, and that really limits what we can do right now. I understand his reasoning, but concrete won't set below forty degrees. Well, the highs are in the twenties. We're stuck doing interior work for now. We don't have a choice. The interiors are going to be finished well before it warms up enough to get the exterior of all of the pool walls built. But he won't listen."

"I agree, it's a really good idea. Just let me know if you can't make it tomorrow before lunch, and we'll change the time."

"No, tomorrow works. I've spent the last week boxing up stuff, and I can start bringing some of it over. I'd actually feel better about it since my current landlord is really making me uncomfortable about the whole thing."

"Well, Jackson isn't in my county, but let me know if you have any problems with him. I'll call the sheriff over there and have him deal with your landlord if you need me to."

"I really appreciate it, Jacob. I'll let you get out of the cold. I need to head back to Sulfur Springs anyway. I'm going to be cutting out early for the next week to move, so I'd better go and warn Denver. He'll have to get used to dealing with my crew foreman."

"Better you than me. It's bad enough having to deal with Andrews and Jeffries. At least Seth is a little better now that he and Jill are living together. He throws a fit every time they have different schedules. And I'm almost positive I'm going to be looking for a new station receptionist within a year, so I've already asked the county to start looking."

"Yeah, I'll take dealing with Denver over what you're stuck with. Thanks again, Jacob," I said as I extended my hand. We both needed to get out of the cold, and it was time to head back to Sulfur Springs.

"See you tomorrow, Collin," Jacob said as he shook my hand, and we both descended the stairs and headed toward our trucks.

I was too excited to not share my news with my best friend, so I gave Daniel a call before I'd even fully backed out of the driveway.

"Wow, it's the middle of the day, so I know you have news. We don't usually chat until evening."

"Well hello to you, too. Daniel, guess what."

"You're not moving back to California?"

My happiness deflated a little at the sadness in my brother's voice. "Yeah, I really think my place is here in Wyoming."

"Then I'm happy for you, Collin. Did you find a place to live?"

"Yeah, I did. I'm signing the paperwork tomorrow, and I can start moving in tomorrow night. I'll spend the next week or so moving all of my stuff, and then we'll see how things go. I have the option to buy the place if I want, and I've already told him I was interested, but he said to hold off for a month or two for when I wasn't so rushed and see how I feel about the place. It's really nice, Daniel. And it's about the perfect size. I'm excited to finally have some place I won't have to deal with a shitty landlord."

"How do you know your new landlord won't be shitty?"

"Well, he's the sheriff of Crooked Bend, and he just married Sean's brother-in-law. I think if he was going to be a shitty landlord, I'd know."

"Valid point. So when do you need my help to move stuff?"

"You don't have to do that. I know Sean and Jasper will help. They did before. And I can always get some of the crew to help, too."

"Nope. Not happening. I haven't seen you in over a year. When do you need me there?"

"I get the keys tomorrow, so whenever. I'm going to start moving my stuff in tomorrow night."

"I'll be there as soon as I can, then."

"So you're still not back to work?"

"Nope, I'm taking more time off. I'll drop Optimus and Fritz off with Uncle Rourke, and then I'll be on my way to you. I'll bring my truck, and we'll get you moved before the weekend is over. I'll probably crash at your place for a few days, if that works?"

"Yeah, sounds great. I'll call you tonight when I get home. I have to get back to work. But I want to talk more, all right?"

"Yep," Daniel said before he ended the call. There was definitely something going on with my brother, and I needed to find out what. But that would have to wait until tonight. For now, I had to deal with Denver and his overall asshole self.

Dalton — 6

When you were stuck working weekends, it didn't matter that you didn't have anyone in your life or not. But what did matter—especially on a Sunday morning—was good coffee. And if I was lucky, coffee cake to go with it.

I never got to talk to Collin because he didn't come back to the station to sign the paperwork. I guess Jacob had taken it out to him, or he'd gone out to their ranch or something. I knew I needed to talk to him and actually exchange phone numbers this time because I couldn't get the man out of my thoughts. Especially since the chemistry between the two of us was definitely there. It was off the charts, and I'd never had it like that with anyone before. Unfortunately, Jacob was being tight-lipped about Collin, but luckily for me, I knew where his house in town was. I just needed to swing by and see if I could catch him there.

"Hey, Deputy Andrews. What can I get for you this morning, hotness?" I did a double take at the guy behind the cash register. I almost didn't even recognize him, but it was the flirting that gave him away.

"Hawke, what the hell happened to your hair?" Before he answered, loud laughter sounded from the side of the room, and I looked over to see none other than Collin. Unfortunately, he wasn't alone. The dark-haired brick house he was with had stopped laughing until Collin whispered something, and then he looked at the blond and smiled. Damn. They definitely knew each other.

I turned my attention back to the young man behind the counter, who was glaring at me. *What'd I do now?* His hair was going to take some getting used to because I'd only ever seen it when it was almost white. But the light brown looked better with his tan complexion.

"What?" I asked innocently.

"Don't what me. If you must know, I had to stop bleaching my hair when it started falling out. This is pretty close to my natural color. What can I get you? Your usual?"

"Yes, please. And can I get an extra coffee cake to go?"

"You'll have to wait on that one. They're in the oven. Collin took all but one of them. It doesn't look like they've eaten them all though. Maybe you can get him to give up one of the ones I wrapped up for him."

"No, that's fine. I can swing back by later and grab one. Will you keep one set aside for me? And when did you guys start opening on Sunday?"

"Yes, I can. And when Rhett stepped way back from working the bakery so much himself, he made me and Cody managers. We split the week between us and work every other day and have each hired a full-time person and a part-time person. It works out really well, and now we're open seven days a week."

"I guess I didn't even realize. That's great though. Especially since I work rotating days."

"Yeah. Just show up before four, and we'll have fresh coffee for you if you want it. If you're looking for a baked good of some sort, you might want to make sure you're here before two."

"Good to know," I said as I handed over my bank card. Now that I was done chatting with Hawke, I really needed to get out of there before I said something I'd regret to Collin. Once Hawke handed me my coffee and cake, I turned to leave but stopped short when I almost collided with Collin.

"Hey, Dalton. Can I talk to you for a few? Or are you in a hurry to get back to work? I didn't realize you wore a Stetson. It looks good on you," he rambled.

Hawke could be heard giggling behind me, and I turned and glared at the him.

"Yeah, I have a few. What's up?"

"Do you want to sit down? Or not?"

"I probably shouldn't. I don't want to intrude."

"Oh, it's not an intrusion. Daniel would like to meet you anyway. I might have mentioned you a time or two to him over the past several days. But I really feel I need to apologize again. I truly am sorry. I never meant to hurt you the way I did."

Collin was really sincere with his apology, and maybe I'd been too harsh on him. We all made mistakes. Hell, it wasn't like I hadn't done exactly what he'd said, *after* I'd realized I *had* made a mistake. But still, did I want to meet the newest love interest?

"Apology accepted. But I don't feel that joining you is for the best."

"Okay. So does that mean there's no chance of me buying you dinner? Daniel is going back to California on Wednesday or Thursday, so I'll be free next weekend."

"Yeah, I don't really think so, Collin. I'm…let's just leave it at the one night, all right?"

"No, it's not all right. I can't…yeah, I get it. I won't bug you again, Deputy. Have a good day."

I watched as Collin made his way back to the table in the corner. It hurt to watch him go, but really, what did he expect? He'd already moved on, and I was too damn old to be an occasional hookup. That wasn't what I was looking for, and I had started to think he felt the same way. Obviously not, and wasn't that just my luck.

I took my purchases and left the bakery in hopes of being able to concentrate on my tasks I needed to get done. I wasn't holding my breath though. And if Collin was moving to the town I worked in, that just meant I'd probably run into him more often than I wanted.

"I didn't expect you back so soon," Jacob said as I walked in the door. I reached down and gave Daisy an ear scratch when she came to greet me. I'd only been gone just a few minutes, but you'd never know by the way she was always so happy to see me.

"Hey, girl," I told her before looking at my boss. "I didn't expect you at work today. It's Sunday—what are you doing here? Why aren't you home with your new husband?"

"I'll get there in a little bit. He's actually at the store picking up some things for Mack, who's with my mom for a bit. I have some paperwork that has to be submitted to the county by tomorrow, so I need to get it finished. We're going to help Collin and Daniel move the last of his furniture, but I need to get this paperwork finished first."

"Oh. I thought I did all of the paperwork for you. And you know Daniel?"

"You did a lot of it. But this is for the position of chief deputy. I have to put in my nomination and fill out the paperwork. And yes, we all know Daniel. He was on the team that helped find Rhett when he was kidnapped a couple years ago."

"Oh, I didn't know that. I mean, I knew about Rhett's kidnapping, but not who all helped find him. I feel bad for him, but he seems to be doing okay now. Paperwork is never fun—sorry, man. Do you know when the new personnel will start arriving?"

"I was told next week. We'll see though."

"Sounds good. If you need anything, just let me know."

"Will do," Jacob said before he disappeared back into his office.

I didn't think anything of what Jacob had said until later on that day at home. I'd already gone through the normal evening dinner routine with Knight, and Daisy had spent time out in the corral with him. Never did I expect her to take to the ranch like she did, but she loved it out here. And when she was at the station with me, she lounged on her bed I'd bought her and put beside my desk. Jacob laughed and shook his head, but I noticed he brought treats for her on a regular basis.

But there was something nagging me about what Jacob had said earlier. Everyone knew Daniel. So did that mean that he and Collin were already an item? Did Collin cheat with me? Shit. I hated this. Needing to have an answer but still not having Collin's number, I made sure Daisy was comfortable, and then I headed into Crooked Bend. If I'd just gotten his phone number, I could have texted him, but nope, I hadn't made it that far yet.

When I pulled up in front of what I knew was Jacob's house in town, I saw a familiar black truck, but it was beside another black truck that had California tags on it. But I already knew to expect him to be there. Should I leave it alone or confront him? Knowing I'd never be able to leave it alone, I got out of the truck.

"Fuck it. I need to let him know how I feel about our situation," I muttered to myself as I walked up the front steps and rang the doorbell. Never did I expect to be met with a half-dressed Daniel. Shit, I didn't stand a chance. His muscles had muscles. When I'd called him a brick house earlier, I was spot-on.

"Hey, Dalton. Collin is in the shower, but come on in. We're waiting for pizza. You want a beer?"

How exactly did he know who I was? Would Collin have told him about me? "No—thanks though. I can come back another time. I should have known…" I trailed off when Collin appeared in the doorway and stopped.

"Dalton. I wasn't expecting you."

"Yeah, sorry about that. There was something I needed to talk to you about, and I didn't have your number."

"Dude, put a shirt on. I've been trying to get a date with him, and I'm not going to stand a chance now that he's seen you, you dolt."

"So much love. I'm wounded. Do you see what I have to put up with? And after I came all this way to help him move, too."

Daniel placed his hand over his heart but quickly moved it to catch the shirt that Collin had ran upstairs to get him.

I volleyed between the two—it was obvious they were close. Of course they were. I'd finally found a guy that tied me up in knots, and of course he'd be taken. That's how life worked. I'd spent thirty-five years alone. Now that I was looking for something more serious, the guy already had…what? A fuck buddy? An open relationship?

"What did you want to talk to me about? And if you want, I'll gladly give you my number. Just give me your phone." Collin held out his hand, and thankfully, I was saved by the doorbell ringing.

"Pizza's here!" Daniel said as he squeezed by me. Collin gave me one of his killer smiles, the same one that got me into this entire mess.

"You want to stay for dinner? Jasper said he was picking up six pizzas. There should be plenty. Even with Daniel and how much he can eat."

"I should probably go. I knew you were moving and had company. I just…"

"Dalton, what's going on? You keep running off and basically avoiding me."

"Dude, he's not interested; you've said it yourself," Daniel said as he came back through the doorway. The look of hurt that Collin couldn't mask made me mad.

"I love you, Daniel, but you're an ass sometimes. Thanks for rubbing it in my face that I can't catch a decent guy," Collin said before he ran off toward the stairs.

"Shit. I'm really sorry, Dalton. He's talked about you all week. I don't know what you two have going on, but you've got my big bro in a mess. I've never seen him like this. Not even over the last guy, and they were together for over a year. Let me go fix it if I can," Daniel said before he chased after Collin. That left me standing in the middle of the kitchen, dumbfounded, with the two guys who'd brought pizza and who knew what else.

"Collin loves all of his brothers, but he and Daniel have always been close, from what I've heard. I don't think we've ever been formally introduced. I'm Jasper, and this is my husband, Liam. My brother and I work with Collin."

"Nice to meet you. Brothers, you say? So they're not together?"

Liam giggled at that, and I could see why Jasper had a thing for his husband. He was cute, but not my type. Blond I obviously had no problems with. But I was over six foot, and I loved it that Collin was still taller than me. His build was a little slimmer, but I also knew I wasn't going to hurt him in the bedroom.

"Yeah, Collin is the oldest. They have a brother between them, and then one that's younger than Daniel. Collin looks like their mom, and Daniel and the other two look like their dad," Jasper told me.

"Would you two excuse me for a minute?"

"Sure," Jasper said as he set the pizza boxes down on the counter. I took off for the stairs, and it wasn't too difficult to find my target. He and Daniel were arguing in the bedroom at the end of the hallway. I didn't even knock; I just walked into the bedroom. They both stopped and looked at me.

"Daniel, would you give us a minute? Please?"

"Sure," he said as he walked past me. I walked right up to Collin and wrapped my arms around his waist. He gave me a confused look but placed his hands on my shoulders.

"He's your brother? And not your boyfriend?"

"What? Who? Daniel? Eewww. Yeah, he's my younger brother. He's about two and a half years younger than me. Lucas is between us. Our parents popped out four boys in no time. What's going on, Dalton?"

"Have dinner with me. You've tied me up in knots, Collin, and I need to know where this is going between us." I didn't give Collin time to answer before I covered his mouth with mine, desperately needing a taste of him again. It'd been over two weeks since I'd kissed him, and that was entirely too long.

He tasted exactly like I remembered, and I couldn't get enough of him. Thankfully, Collin had enough sense to break from the kiss though.

"As much as I want to continue this—preferably naked and in my bed—I have company downstairs, and I really don't want them to know what we're doing up here."

"Shit. Sorry. I just…every time I'm around you, my brain seems to stop working."

"How about dinner? I know there's enough pizza, because not only was Jasper bringing pizza, so are Sean and Simon."

"You mean there's more coming?"

The doorbell chiming let me know that the rest of his company had arrived.

"Dinner? And dammit, give me your number already," Collin said before slamming his mouth down on mine again.

Collin — 7

I loved my brother. I honestly did. Out of all of my brothers and cousins, I was closest to Daniel. But it was past time for him to go home. Dalton and I had either talked to each other or texted every day since Sunday, and I was past ready to go out on a date with him, but Daniel was still hanging around. That let me know that something was up—seriously up—and I needed to find out what was bothering my brother.

"Daniel? You've been here for a week now. What's up? I know you came to help me move, but it's more than that. So what gives?"

"My last assignment got to me, that's all. I'm taking some extended time off."

"You want to talk about it?"

"Not really, no. But it's made me think a lot about my job and what we've been doing. Don't get me wrong, what Taylor and James have going is great; they help so many people. But my last assignment was overseas, and it wasn't pretty. It got me thinking, and I just don't know anymore."

"Don't know what?"

"Honestly, what I want to do with my life. I thought I had it figured out, but I'm second-guessing myself now. And there's some other things I'm adjusting to."

"Okay, one issue at a time, what do you mean you're second-guessing yourself?"

"It's just like you. You've finally decided that maybe Wyoming is where you were meant to be. I mean, you're a partner in the firm now. That's no small potatoes. And even I can admit that your guy is easy on the eyes."

"Okay, let's jump to that real quick because you just blushed—and Daniel, you *never* blush. What's going on?"

"You've always known you were gay, right?"

"Yeah. Is that what this is about?"

"A little, yeah. I mean, you know I've only ever been with women. But after our last mission I met this guy, things happened, and before I knew it, we were in bed together. Best sex of my life, too. So I guess I'm bi?"

"Wow. Okay. You know I don't have a problem with that, right? And neither will Uncle Rourke. No matter what, he's going to love and accept you. Hell, Travis is his son, and there's no denying that Travis is gay. After our parents were killed, you *know* we became his. Uncle Rourke loves us just as much as he loves his own boys."

"I know. And I'm so thankful for that. But I mean, I've spent all this time thinking I was one thing, when I'm possibly not."

"Okay. Question for you. Do you think that maybe it was just situational? That maybe you two turned to each other because of what happened? You never did say who it was."

"I'd really rather not say who it was. And I thought about that. About it being because of the situation. It's not."

"So you and he…"

"No. Only the once. I went to a club in California and…let's just say that I didn't go home alone that night."

"All right. And are you having problems with the fact that you're into guys?"

"No. Not at all. It's just made me stop and think about different things. And honestly, it's made certain things make more sense."

"Like why you couldn't quite commit to Libby?"

"Yeah, exactly that. But after that last assignment, I'm wondering if maybe I should look for a new career. I'm not the only one that feels this way either. But I feel…"

"What? You know I've never asked about your job. I know you work in security of some sort, but that's about all I know. I know you travel out of the country a lot. But this sounds like more than that."

"Yeah, I run the rescue ops division of Stealth Securities. And we were sent on a mission to rescue a client's kid. It wasn't pretty at all."

"Okay, I don't need to know any more details unless you feel I do. So what…you quit?"

"No, just took a leave of absence. I needed some time off. And it's really made me remember how much I love working with dogs."

"Well, I'm sure there's plenty you can do with dogs and still work in that line of work. I don't know, couldn't you train them for security or something?"

"I've thought about it. It's something they don't currently do though."

"There's always starting your own business. Or maybe…I don't know. Why didn't you say something sooner?"

"Because I've had fun watching a certain deputy turn you into mush."

"Shut up. He has not." When Daniel raised his eyebrow at me and looked at me in disbelief, I rethought my answer. "Okay, maybe. But you know it's taken me a long time after what Carter did to even contemplate talking to another guy, let alone sleeping with him."

"I know. And I still say that you need to let me go find Carter and talk to him."

"I don't need you getting into trouble because of me."

"I'd have to get caught to get into trouble."

I rolled my eyes at my brother, who laughed. "You're a mess."

"True. But you love me."

"I do. But you're still a mess."

"Don't worry. Me and my mess will be out of your hair tomorrow. I know I'm cramping your style and all that."

"You are not."

"Really? Is that why you haven't gone out with your guy?"

"No. We've both been busy. You know that. And besides, how do you know I haven't gone out with him?"

"Well, you come home every evening after work. So I know you haven't gone out with him. And he hasn't come over for dinner or anything."

"He's been busy working. I talk to him every day."

"Well, now you'll be able to do more than talk. I'll be out of your hair tomorrow. I need to get home anyway. My babies miss me."

I had to laugh at that. But he was probably right about it on some level. They probably did miss him. Daniel doted on his dogs, and they were glued to his side every time I'd ever seen them together.

"Don't feel you have to leave."

"I don't. But I might come back sometime. Maybe I'll bring the dogs with me. Can you have dogs here? You know they're not destructive."

"Yeah, I can. Especially since I'm going to buy the place."

"You still thinking about that?"

"Nope. I've decided."

"Yeah, but doesn't the deputy live somewhere else?"

"He does. But what's that have to do with anything?"

"Nothing, I guess. I just figured that maybe you'd…"

"Nope. Not happening. I lived with Carter, remember? I don't want to go through that shit again."

"Not everyone is a closeted asshole, Collin. And if you think about it, Dalton didn't ignore you that night when he was here when we were moving you in."

"I get that. But we just met, okay?"

"Whatever you say. But I've seen how he looks at you. He's got 'commitment' written all over him. And you were a mess all week last week."

"Okay, time to change the subject. Let's talk about something else."

"Got it. You're uncomfortable. But I'm headed to bed anyway. So you can go to your room and call your guy that isn't anything serious, and I'm going to sleep. I want to leave stupid early because I'm not planning on stopping on the way home. Are you coming home for Christmas? You know Uncle Rourke is going to ask."

"I was thinking about it. I'll let you know in another week or so. It really depends on things with the project I'm working on and where it's at."

"You don't give your guys time off? That's harsh."

"We've been talking about shutting down all projects between Christmas and New Year's. We're still talking about it though. I'll have an answer for you by December," I told Daniel, and he nodded. I was glad that was an acceptable answer. I watched my brother walk down the hallway and then start to climb the stairs. I was really worried about him but didn't know what I could do to help. But the fact he'd already opened up to me was reassuring. Except he waited until the night before he was leaving. I was about to chase after him, but Dalton picked that exact moment to text me.

Dalton: Hey, you busy?

Me: Nope. What's up?

Dalton: Can you talk?

Me: Yep.

My phone immediately rang in my hand, and I smiled at the prospect of talking to Dalton. It'd been a couple of days since we'd actually had a chance to talk to each other.

"Hey, I'm going crazy. Say you can meet me for coffee tomorrow morning?"

"Well, hello to you, too, Deputy."

"Backstreet, I'm serious here. I haven't seen you since Sunday."

"Backstreet? What the hell?"

"Well, you look like you belong in one of those boy bands. You know…like that group that Justin Timberlake used to be in."

"Okay, that was *NSYNC, not the Backstreet Boys."

"The real issue here is that you know who they both are and aren't. So the nickname fits."

"Whatever, asshole."

"That I've more than earned. I'll accept that as my nickname. Now, coffee. Tomorrow. You have to work at some point, right?"

"Dalton, I've been working all week. What are you talking about?"

"Yeah, but your brother is there, right?"

"Yeah, he's leaving tomorrow morning. He's going through a lot right now."

"Now I really do feel like an asshole."

"Don't. He didn't bother to tell me about any of it until about fifteen minutes ago. So, coffee?"

"Yes. You, me, Son of a Biscuit. I'm off tomorrow and I'd love to have coffee with you. And if that goes well—and you're free and willing—we could maybe have dinner tomorrow night? I can take care of Knight early and then take you out if that works."

"That sounds acceptable," I replied while trying to not laugh out loud. I was almost successful. Almost. I lost it when Dalton replied though.

"Really? That sounds acceptable? Really? If it's such a hardship to go out with me, I'll withdraw the offer."

"Don't you dare. I'd love to have coffee. And dinner. What time?"

"Just give me a text when you get up and you know when your brother is going to leave. I'll head over that way."

"You know, why don't I head your way? I'm in Sulfur Springs six days a week, you know. There's that coffeehouse there. What's it called?"

"The Brew Crew? Yeah, we can do that. But it doesn't have coffee cake."

I rolled my eyes. He was actually pouting. "Dalton, how many days a week do you eat coffee cake?"

"When Hawke has it. Why?"

"You're just as bad as Rhett's husband, Logan, about his pumpkin scones."

"Do you blame him? Have you tasted those things?"

"Yes, I have. I've watched Rhett put the icing on them when they were still warm."

Dalton groaned and I realized two things about him in that moment. One, he had a major sweet tooth, and two, him groaning about baked goods turned me on. Shit, I was in trouble.

"Okay, that was just mean. So tomorrow?"

"Yes. Aside from work, I'll be completely yours until you tell me it's time to go home."

"And if I ask you to stay?"

That was the big question, wasn't it? Damn, I wanted Dalton again, but would it mess things up? I really liked him. He made me actually feel things, and when I looked into his blue eyes…yeah.

"Backstreet?"

"Huh?"

"Where'd you go?"

"Nowhere. I was thinking about what you said."

"Hey, we don't have to. I just want dinner. Okay? We haven't really had much of a chance to get to know each other. I'd really like to see if this could go anywhere."

"No, I agree. And I wasn't saying I wasn't interested. Because I am. I really am. But I don't want to mess anything up."

"We'll figure it out. Text me tomorrow, and I'll head over to the Brew and Crew and meet you for coffee before you head to work."

"Yeah, that works for me. I'm not sure when it'll be though, okay?"

"Don't worry about it. I'll be up. Daisy doesn't know how to sleep in, and Knight always needs to be taken care of."

"You're sure? And who's Knight?"

"Positive. Knight is my horse. I finally have a place and time for him and I'm thankful for that. So I'll see you tomorrow?"

"You will. Have a good night, okay?"

"You too." Dalton ended the call before I could reply again. I had an idea and hoped like hell that Jacob would be a willing accomplice. Thankfully, he was more than willing to give me Dalton's address when I texted him asking for it. I just had to promise to *fix* his deputy. Whatever the hell that meant.

Dalton — 8

I was just about to call Collin when there was a knock on my front door. Daisy, of course, beat me there, but like the good girl she was, she sat patiently waiting for me to open the door so she could see who had come to visit her. Because she was positive that everyone who came out to the place was there to see her.

Never did I expect to see a certain architect on the other side of the door, holding a familiar bag from a bakery in Crooked Bend.

"You mentioned coffee cake. Hawke is working this morning, so I swung by and picked up a couple. You have coffee, right?"

I stepped back and let Collin in out of the cold. Immediately, he knelt down and gave Daisy hugs and ear scratches.

"What are you doing here?"

"I thought you wanted to have coffee?"

"Yeah, but I was going to meet you in town."

"Well, now you don't have to. But if you're uncomfortable with me being here, I can leave. I can't stay long anyway. Denver is in fine form and has already texted me several times this morning."

"Okay, who's Denver and why is he texting you?"

"He's Hawke's brother. And he's texting me because I'm working on a project out at his ranch."

"Oh. Can you stay long enough for coffee?"

"That was the plan, yes. And maybe you'd be nice enough to share one of those coffee cakes."

I hugged the bag to my chest, which earned me a laugh from Collin.

"Come here, you," I said as I pulled him up to his feet. When he was standing up, I wrapped my arms around him, and then life was blissful. His lips were on mine once again, and when our tongues dueled for dominance, I gave in and let him own the kiss. That was a smart call on my part. The things he could do with his tongue. I couldn't wait to reacquaint myself with what else he was capable of.

"Okay, I swear I didn't come here for a quickie. I've never really been a fan of those, but I'm beginning to reconsider my way of thinking."

"Nope. No quickies. I need more coffee. Come with me," I said as I tugged on Collin's hand and led him into the kitchen. We spent almost an hour drinking coffee and eating the coffee cake he'd brought. I couldn't wait to see where things went after dinner. I just had to keep myself occupied until later.

Reluctantly, I kissed Collin goodbye and watched him climb in his truck and drive away. I wasn't planning on doing much of anything, except cleaning up in case I somehow managed to talk Collin into spending the night. But that plan got waylaid when I got a call from Jacob. I sent Collin a text, letting him know I was headed into work for a bit, but it shouldn't interfere with our evening plans.

"Dalton, thanks for coming in. I know it's your day off, but I wanted to talk to you about something."

"Sure, Jacob. What's up?" I asked as I followed him into the office and sat down in a chair across from his desk.

"You remember when I was in here because I had to finish some paperwork for chief deputy?"

"Yeah. What of it?"

"I didn't want to say anything until I knew the results. The county made their decision, and they agreed with my nomination."

"That's great. So who did you nominate?"

"You, silly. Why else would I bring you in to talk about this?"

"What? You nominated me? Why me?"

"Are you not happy about it? I thought you would be. You seemed really happy here. Hell, you were the one who called me asking if I really was looking for more deputies when you wanted to work here."

"Yeah, but that was just as a deputy. I never thought you'd consider me for chief deputy. I haven't even been here that long."

"I know, but you aren't without experience. I mean, you already came in as a captain. You're kinda skipping a few ranks here, so I thought you'd jump at it."

"Yeah, but that was with the Denver PD. Not the Crooked Bend sheriff department."

"So, are you turning down the position?"

"Hell no. Give me the paperwork. Where do I sign? I get two days a week off now, right?"

Jacob laughed while handing over the paperwork. If I could wrangle a second day off, I'd have more time to spend with Knight. I couldn't exactly bring him to the station with me like I did Daisy.

"Yeah, a second day off is in the works. We're getting in newbies starting today. I'm trying not to cringe about the prospect, but it can't be helped."

"That's the understatement of the year. I don't know how you did it all alone. That's just insane."

"Yeah, life was hell then. I have three of you now, and it's still not enough. But you'll soon find out, there's nothing fast when it comes to the county."

"Oh, I already knew that. So, what's the plan?"

"Well, you'll move your shit into the other office and give one of the new guys your desk. And hopefully, we can get enough personnel in here that we're not all working close to eighty hours a week. I swear, sometimes I get up before Isaac, and he gets up crazy early to go take care of all of the horses at the ranch."

"How's married life treating you?"

"It's great. You should try it."

I shrugged at that. I wasn't against marriage, but I wasn't running out looking for rings anytime soon. I'd watched my parents make each other a laughingstock for most of my life, and it really made me hesitant to run out and get married. That didn't mean I wasn't looking for commitment, or even marriage, if the right guy came along and the timing was right.

"Okay, well, I see I get a nice pay raise with the new position as well. Not that I had much of a complaint about the current pay."

"Yeah, I know it's not a lot, but it's better than nothing."

"Did you not read the paperwork? It's a good pay jump."

"Yeah, I read it. I'm glad you're on board. Now, if you'd go clean out your desk, I'd appreciate it. I really need the space. And Jeffries is supposed to help me rearrange the desks so we can bring in a couple more. They're scheduled to be delivered this afternoon."

"I can stick around and help if you'd like. I didn't have anything planned except cleaning."

"You sure?"

"Yeah. Daisy should be good for a few hours, at least. And if nothing else, I could see if Collin could swing by and let her out. He mentioned something about being stuck at Knotty Springs Ranch. I didn't realize it was about ten minutes from my place."

"Oh yeah? He called me last night asking for your address. I hope it was okay I gave it to him."

"So that's how he got it. Yeah. It's fine. He showed up this morning with coffee cake. I'll never turn that down."

Jacob chuckled as I walked out of the office and made my way to my new office. I guess the paper on the window that was covering the new vinyl lettering with my name as the new chief should have been a giveaway that we were getting a new one. I just never thought it'd be me. I opened the office and had to admit it wasn't going to be a hardship to have my own office. There was plenty of room for Daisy's bed over behind the desk, so that was the first thing I moved. An hour later, my new office was set up, and I realized I definitely needed more stuff. The place looked barren compared to Jacob's office.

"Hey, Andrews. You're the new chief, huh?" Gavin asked as he came in and sat in the chair on the other side of my desk.

"Cruz, what're you doing here? Don't you work the evening shift tonight?"

"Nope. Jeffries is staying late. He's pouting because of Jill."

I groaned. Those two were going to be the death of the entire department. "What now?"

"I wish I knew. I guess they had a fight or something, and she called Jacob and asked for some time off because she needed to 'figure things out.' Whatever the hell that means. I mean, she married Seth after what, a couple months? They really rushed things for being as young as they are."

"I guess, yeah. I don't know. If you know, you know. But what could those two be arguing about already?"

"Not sure. You need to go shopping or something. There's not a lot in here."

"I was just thinking about that when you poked your head in. I have some stuff packed up at home. I'll bring it in. But I might need to go shopping as well. What time is it?"

"Almost noon, why?"

"Shit, really?"

"Yeah. Forget your watch or something?"

"Actually, yeah. But I'm sure Daisy needs out. Give me a sec."

Me: Hey, can you do me a huge favor?

Collin: Sure. What?

Me: I'm still at the office. Can you run over to the ranch and let Daisy out? The door on the backside of the garage is unlocked.

Collin: Sure. I'm actually on lunch break right now. I'll run over and let her out. Do I need to do anything else for her?

Me: No, she probably just needs to pee. Thanks, Collin.

Collin: No problem. We still on for tonight?

Me: Yes. See you at six?

Collin: Yep. TTYL

"Do I want to know?"

"What?"

"You have a goofy look on your face."

"Do not."

"Wanna bet?"

"No. I needed to see if Collin could run over and let Daisy out. She hasn't been out since this morning. I didn't think I'd be here this long, or I would have brought her with me."

"Gotcha. Okay, well now that our mascot is taken care of, you can come help move desks."

"Sounds like a plan," I said as I got up and followed Gavin out of the office.

By three, I was finally home and looking forward to a long hot shower. The last thing I expected was to find my dog missing.

Me: Did you let Daisy back in when you left?

Collin: Nope. She was whining and sitting at my truck door and wouldn't go back inside. She's over here with me. I hope that's okay. I didn't want to just leave her outside. Seriously. She wouldn't go back in the house.

Ugh. That's all I needed. A dog that became overly attached to a guy that might or might not be willing to stick around. I hoped like hell he was though.

Me: No, it's fine. So, still on for six?

Collin: Yep. I'll probably be a little early. We usually knock off at five and are out of here by a quarter after. I should be there before half past. That okay?

Me: Yep. See you then.

Shit. I had under three hours to get the place cleaned up and ready for the possibility of having an overnight guest. I really needed to take care of Knight, but it was too early. Opting for several showers today, I hopped in and took a quick one before I pulled on clean jeans and a flannel shirt. I changed the sheets and stuffed the dirty ones in the washer before starting it and then going to see what I had to feed Collin. It didn't look promising, so we would probably have to go out. That was okay, I could work with that. But it also meant I had to hustle and get Knight taken care of. I'd have to check on him again after dinner, but that was doable, so I headed out to the stables to let my boy out. I really missed riding him, but I just didn't have time at the moment. The snow on the ground didn't help either. It made things a little difficult and sometimes treacherous.

After his stall was clean and he was fed, happily eating a very early dinner, I headed back inside for another shower. I really didn't expect to see Collin's truck parked beside my house. I didn't even hear it pull up.

"Hey. I was just going to head out there looking for you," Collin said as he came up to me for a kiss.

"I'm in desperate need of a shower, so you might not want to get too close."

"What a coincidence. So am I," Collin said as he wrapped his arms around me and kissed me anyway. I knew there was no way he was covered in manure, but he didn't seem to care. The man could kiss, and when his lips landed on mine, it was still the same. My mind went blank, and my body tingled.

"I'm supposed to be taking you out to dinner."

"You can take me out to dinner. After we shower," Collin said as he grabbed my hand and pulled me into the house. Daisy was fast asleep on her bed in the living room beside the fireplace and didn't even look up when we walked by and climbed the stairs. What was wrong with me? Collin was here and wanted to shower with me. Why would I tell him no?

Collin — 9

I'd spent well over a year without having sex after I left Alabama and moved to Wyoming. I'd wanted absolutely nothing to do with sex and men, period. Then one night with Dalton, and I couldn't get enough. It'd taken me three weeks to get close to him again, and if he didn't push me away, I was going to see how far I could get him to go.

"Collin, wait." Dammit. I knew that tone. So much for getting lucky. Fuck. My. Life.

"No, Dalton. I don't want to wait. If we wait, you'll talk us out of doing what we both want to do." I stopped halfway up the stairs and turned to look at him. "Really? Fine. I'll head home and shower. If you still want to take me out to dinner, you know where I live."

"What? Wait! What is wrong with you? Why are you always jumping to conclusions where I'm concerned?" Dalton followed me down the stairs but stopped me in the living room before I could make it to the door. "I was only going to ask if you had clean clothes or not. But now, I really think it might be best if you do go home and shower. We can still do dinner if you want, but maybe we should do that another night as well. Maybe one where you're a little more reasonable."

"Reasonable? Really?"

"Yes. Have you listened to yourself? First, you thought I had skipped out on you, and now you think…I don't know what you're thinking. Why would I talk you out of doing what we both want? Collin, you're not going to like it, but maybe you should go. We don't really seem to be able to get into a good routine. I thought we were making headway, but I'm too damn old for this shit."

"What shit?"

"The immature reactions to situations."

"Did you really just call me immature?"

"Hey, if the shoe fits."

"You're an asshole."

"Tell me something I haven't heard before. I tell it like it is, and if you can't handle that, then we have no future."

"Tell me something. When you saw me at the wedding, did you think 'future' or did you think 'fuck buddy'?" I waited for an answer, and when I didn't get one, I turned and left. I really didn't have the desire to figure out the hot-and-cold moods that Dalton seemed to have. I climbed into my truck and went home. By the time I arrived back in Crooked Bend, I was even more pissed off, and I quickly sent a text to Dalton.

Me: Forget dinner. Actually, just forget my number, period.

Dalton: If that's the way you want it. I'm sorry.

I needed a shower and a beer, at the very least. So I climbed the stairs and stripped and threw my clothes in the direction of the hamper. Half of them made it, but I simply didn't care. I was in a mood and wasn't concerned where my clothes landed. After a long hot shower, I dried off and pulled on a pair of sweats. I retrieved my phone from where I'd tossed it on the bed and went downstairs to find something for dinner.

After checking the sparse contents of my refrigerator, I decided I'd have to get dressed and head to the diner or order pizza. Nope. Cereal it was. After devouring half a box of Lucky Charms, I decided to give my brother a call. He picked up as I was flopping down on my couch.

"I'm not even home yet. Something has to be wrong."

"What do you mean you're not home yet? You left before the sun came up."

"Yeah, but it's only been a little over twelve hours. What's wrong, Collin?"

"Am I immature?"

At Daniel's laugh, I knew there was probably some substance to Dalton's accusation.

"Oh man, I really like Dalton now. I take it he's the reason you asked?"

"Shut up. I'm sorry I called you. I'm going to bed. When you see Uncle Rourke, tell him I'm coming home for Christmas and to pick me up at the airport."

"Don't tease, Collin. If you're here, we'll all be here."

"Not teasing. There's no reason for me to be here. Dalton and I aren't going to be seeing each other again."

"I don't buy it. I say, give it not even a week and you'll go out."

"Nope," I said, popping the *p*. I was finished with him. I didn't need another asshole in my life. I'd had that with Carter for too long.

"Okay, whatever you say. I'll let him know. I have to swing by and pick up my babies, so expect a call from him soon."

"Will do. I'm going to go to bed, otherwise I'm just going to mope around the house."

"You could unpack, you know."

"Yeah, but I actually feel like moping. Unpacking is work. I'm not in the mood to work. I spent all damn day working."

"Fine. Go to bed and mope."

"Night, Daniel."

"Hey, Collin?"

"Yeah?"

"It'll work out if it's supposed to."

"Yeah, well, I don't think it's supposed to. We'll see though. Talk to you soon."

Daniel hung up the phone, and I got up off the couch. After checking all the doors, I turned off the lights and climbed the stairs. I loved spending the afternoon with Daisy; maybe I should get a dog, too. Naw, I didn't have time for a dog. Maybe a finicky cat. I got along with my friend's cat, Hemingway, well enough.

I climbed into bed and realized it was only a little after six. If I went to bed now, I'd be up in the middle of the night. Dammit, Daniel was right. I needed to unpack. Hauling my ass back down the stairs, I decided to put some time into the office. I'd set up my drafting table and unpacked my laptop and that was it. I still had boxes of books and other things for the shelves that Daniel had helped me assemble. It'd been great spending time with him; I just needed to figure out how I could help him deal with everything he had going on.

By the time I had finished unpacking the last box, it was almost eleven and time to head to bed, finally. After climbing the stairs, yet again, I brushed my teeth and then flopped down on my bed. Trying to not think about the sexy deputy with the blue eyes that made me want things, I eventually fell into a fitful sleep. That didn't help the next morning when I woke up late for work. I was more than ready to be finished with Denver and his Knotty Springs Ranch. I just hoped like hell he was in a much more mellow mood.

After rushing through my morning routine, I ran out the door and hoped Son of a Biscuit didn't have too long of a line. I really needed coffee and didn't have a bunch of time to wait. Luck was on my side because only two people were in line in front of me. Regrettably, one just so happened to be the man I'd spent the better part of the night trying to not think about.

His ass looked so good in his uniform trousers, and that hat... Damn, when did I develop a thing for cowboy hats? Oh yeah, right about the time I met Dalton Andrews. When he turned, he stopped and gave me a pained look, and I simply nodded at him.

"Deputy. Mornin'," I said as I moved closer to the counter. I started eyeballing the baked goods and hoped that would be the end of any interaction between us. Thankfully, he sighed and then simply left.

"Good morning, Collin. The usual?" Cindy, the other girl who worked behind the counter, asked. That meant that Hawke wasn't here and Cody was. I don't know why Cody insisted on working with Cindy when he had a thing for Angie. But then, I didn't understand much when it came to attraction it seemed.

"Actually, no. Just the coffee please. Thanks," I said as I handed her a five and then tossed a dollar in the tip jar before taking my extra-sweet coffee and leaving. It was way too early, and I hadn't had enough sleep or coffee yet, but I swear I saw

Carter, my ex, across the street. But when I looked again, he wasn't there. Yep, definitely needed more coffee.

After climbing in my truck, I sat and drank some coffee before I headed out of Crooked Bend and toward Sulfur Springs. It really was inconvenient to live in Crooked Bend, but I'd needed a place to live and on short notice. I'd survive commuting. Funny thing was, Jasper was actually closer to the office in Jackson now than I was. Although, only by a few miles, but still. Maybe we should just close the second office and expand the one in Crooked Bend. That was certainly something to bring up.

By the time I pulled across the cattle guard at Knotty Springs, my coffee was gone and I was in a little bit of a better mood. That was until I pulled up to the site. It was never good when I had to deal with a pissed-off Denver first thing in the morning.

"What's wrong, Denver? Girlfriend not put out last night?"

"What my girlfriend and I do and don't do isn't your concern. You're late and your foreman isn't here yet either."

"Nope, and he's not coming in today. He has a very sick kid. I'm not late though because I do have two other projects I'm currently overseeing. You do realize that, right? And I'll bet that even with my foreman not here, the guys are already hard at work."

"That's not the point. Someone should be here to make sure they stay on task."

"Look, Denver. I talked to Hawke, and I understand you're getting a lot of pressure from the girlfriend because she wants a ring and all, but meanwhile, you're alienating not only me, but your little brother as well. Not to mention that Becky doesn't seem to like him."

"Rebecka. Her name is Rebecka. And it's not really any of your concern."

"No? Then go bug her and leave me and my crew alone. Every time you pull one of us off to ask the same question—when will we be finished—you set us that much further behind. I promise, we'll finish much faster if you would just leave us to do our job. There's only so much we can do right now. It's almost Thanksgiving, and we're going to be off from the twenty-eighth until the third. Our crew all have families, and they want to spend time with them. We'll be off over Christmas as well. So just relax and enjoy some time with your brother."

"He annoys Rebecka."

"No, she's insecure and feels threatened by him because you raised him. But you're going to lose your brother if you're not careful."

"What?"

"Denver, when was the last time you talked to Hawke?"

"I don't...he's always gone early and doesn't come back until late, if at all."

"Ever think about the reasoning behind that? Think long and hard about the two people in your life before you choose one over the other. There should be room for both. If not, then maybe you should look for someone who is accepting of your little brother and who he is."

At that, I turned and walked off toward the large stone structure we were working in. It was going to be the main spa, and we were using all-natural stone from the ranch as well as wood that was already cured and was native to the area. The place was truly beautiful, but it was a pain to work with Denver. He hadn't seemed like that much of an ass when I'd first talked to him, but you never could tell with people.

I also knew Hawke had said that Denver had started selling off their livestock. I wasn't so sure that things were stable at Knotty Springs, but Denver had gotten the loan for the construction, so I hoped he was able to make a go of it. If he marketed it correctly, he'd be booked up to a year in advance, and that would be exactly what he needed.

I just hoped he didn't lose his brother along the way. We'd all heard about Becky and how she didn't care for Hawke simply because he actually was better at makeup than she was. Hell, he was better at that stuff than most women actually.

"Jim, how's it going this morning?" I inquired as I walked up to our master electrician.

Dalton — 10

I swear, my life revolved around paperwork. When Jacob put me in for chief, I didn't realize just how much more paperwork I'd be stuck with. But on a brighter note, I didn't have to do patrols anymore. I'd take paperwork over patrols any day. Now if I could just get my private life sorted. I had a horse, I had a dog, and I'd thought I might have a good chance with a man, but shit, that had gone to hell. Maybe I just wasn't meant to have a relationship. I'd refused to when I was with the Denver PD; maybe I should keep it that way.

"Andrews, you sure you want to work Christmas? You worked Thanksgiving," Jacob asked as he came into my office and plopped down. Daisy immediately got up and laid her head in his lap for the required ear rubs.

"I don't mind. I'm single and there's no way in hell I'm going back to Denver to either of my parents' places."

"I thought you and Collin were seeing each other, and I don't know, maybe you were planning on going to California with him."

"Is he going to California?"

"You didn't know?"

"No. Things didn't really work out. I was my usual asshole self, and I haven't talked to him in several weeks. I've tried to call and text him, but he doesn't answer or return my calls."

"You know where he lives, Dalton. What's up?"

"Nothing. It just didn't work out. That's all."

"Okay, well, if you're willing to work Christmas, it's yours. I've now found myself in a much larger, much louder family get-together."

"Yeah, but you knew that going in. You grew up here, right?"

"Yeah. I did. I was friends with Logan and Graham. I've spent so many days out at Wild Creek, I practically lived there."

I smiled at that. Growing up like that would have been nice, but I wasn't that lucky. My parents absolutely hated each other, yet they wouldn't divorce. No, instead, they chose to flaunt their affairs in front of one another. They finally divorced when I was old enough to leave. I joined the police academy right after high school, and I was gone. My dad remarried, and my new step-mom was younger than me and made my dad just as miserable as my mother had, but he was determined to make it work somehow. At least I had something good come from the hell my parents put me through growing up, I knew what *not* to do in a relationship.

"Where'd you go?"

"What? Oh, just thinking about my parents."

"Oh, you planning on—"

"Nope. Not in a million years. I haven't seen either of them in over five years. I like it that way. My dad is miserably married to a woman that is younger than me who doesn't seem to realize I don't have a thing for her, and my mom only whines about how her current boyfriend or her most recent ex treated her. Then she wants me to take her shopping to make her feel better. No, thank you. I'm happier without them in my life."

"Wow. Yeah, I don't blame you. But I was supposed to ask you out to Wild Creek on Sunday. I don't want to hear a no either. It's your day off, so you have no excuses. But Sunday is Rhett's birthday, and they're having a big thing. You're invited. You have a trailer for Knight, right?"

"Yeah, why?"

"Load him up and bring him. You can go out to the arena and ride him around for a couple hours. I know it's not the same as being out on a trail, but it's December twenty-first, it's almost Christmas, and it's cold as all get-out. Don't forget to bring Daisy with you, too. She can play with Ivan."

"Okay, that sounds enticing. I'll be there. What time?"

"It's a lunch thing. I was told eleven. So be there by then, and afterward, you can burn off some of the calories with your horse."

"If you're sure?"

"Absolutely."

"All right, then. I'll be there."

"Good. Now my brother-in-law will get off my back. See you then. I'm headed to my mom's to pick up my son. He spent the day with her and his cousins. I don't know how she does it, actually. I only have one, and he wears me out. She's chasing around four."

"Yeah, that's more than I want. Have fun and I'll see you Sunday."

"Yep. Don't work too hard, Andrews," Jacob said over his shoulder as he left the office. Daisy whined and then went back to her bed and curled back up for another nap. She had tons of toys in the office and spent time either playing or napping. It was a rough life for sure.

I went back to my paperwork and was next interrupted by a knock on the office door.

"Hey, Dalton, Collin is out here, and he needed to talk to Jacob, but he's gone for the day."

"If it's official business, send him in. If not, tell him to call Jacob on his cell."

"It's both, asshole," Collin said as he pushed his way into my office. Daisy jumped up and started whining and yelping like she hadn't seen him in forever. In reality, it had only been about a month. He'd only spent an afternoon with her and look at how she was acting. Not that I blamed her. I'd basically only spent a night with him and I felt the exact same way.

"What can I do for you, Backstreet?"

"Backstreet, really?"

"Well, you referred to me as asshole, so I assumed we were on nickname level. What's up, Collin?"

"When did you make chief? You never told me."

"I didn't get a chance. You left before I could take you to dinner, and you haven't returned any of my calls since."

Collin looked at me like he wanted to say something, but in the end, he chose not to. "So, I'm here for two reasons."

"So you said. Reason one?"

"I'm going out of town tonight, and I'll be gone for a week. I wanted Jacob to know I wouldn't be at the house. I'd appreciate it if he could maybe swing by and check on it once or twice."

"That's a personal thing, so you'll need to call him on his cell."

"Yes and no." Collin held up his hand when I tried to speak, so I let him continue. "About a month ago, I was leaving Son of a Biscuit, and I swore I saw my ex standing across the street. When I grabbed my phone to take a picture, he was gone when I looked again. I put it off as my eyes playing tricks on me. But now I'm almost positive I wasn't seeing things. I swear, I've seen him around in Sulfur Springs multiple times. Here in Crooked Bend as well. And this week, when I've left the jobsite at Knotty Springs, there's been notes under my wiper. They're in his handwriting. Dalton, I think he's stalking me."

It took everything in me to not explode. Instead, I came across as an even bigger asshole. "Name."

"What?"

"Give me the asshole's name."

"Dalton, you're not giving me any warm fuzzies about what you're going to do."

"So help me, Collin, if you don't…"

"Carter Beaumont. But don't do anything you're not supposed to do."

"Do you have a picture? What about the note? You said he'd left you a note."

"He's left several. I have them. Here," Collin said as he handed me a plastic baggie full of notes.

"Fuck. How many are there?"

"Over a dozen. I think my most recent count is fourteen."

"When did they start?"

"This week. On Monday. I've had more than one each day. They just started out with notes saying things like, 'I'm back' or 'I found you' and 'miss me?'. I didn't think about it at all in the beginning, and I touched them. I thought maybe one of the guys left me a note or something. Until I opened it and saw what it was.

I lived with the guy for over a year. I recognize his handwriting, Dalton. And honestly, some of those notes are a little unnerving."

"Give me a second. I need to get some gloves. We'll need to get your prints, too, so we can rule you out. You wouldn't happen to have a picture of the douche, would you? You said you lived with him for over a year."

"I didn't have any pictures of him, no. I grabbed some from social media though and printed them out."

"Smart thinking. I'll be right back," I told Collin as I got up to go grab an evidence kit. I gave Collin's shoulder a little squeeze on my way by, and he grabbed my hand. I stopped long enough to look at him, and the wall I'd put up where he was concerned came tumbling down. This had really shaken him up. I needed to find out more about his ex and why exactly he was an ex.

"Cruz, call Jacob for me, and tell him I need him to come back in. It's really important, and it shouldn't take more than a couple hours."

"On it," Gavin told me as I walked past him and grabbed an evidence bag as well as a fingerprint kit. Gavin nodded at me and gave me a thumbs-up when I walked back by him. He was still on the phone with Jacob, who was only about twenty minutes away, max.

"Collin, you mentioned you were going out of town. Depending on what Jacob thinks, you might need to postpone your trip."

"Okay, but I'll need a good excuse. I don't want my brothers, cousins, or uncle to know about this."

"Why not?"

"They never liked Carter because of what he did, and I'm afraid of what they'll do to him if they find out."

"Okay, what did he do, and am I going to want to kill him?"

"I doubt it. He kept me hidden for our entire relationship. He's deep, deep in the closet. Like, he took a girl to all of his family functions, deep in the closet. I was okay with it at first; I understood. But after a while, when he still didn't come out, I realized he never was going to. That was about the time that Sean and Jasper were looking for another architect. So, I quit my job, broke up with him, and moved. He didn't take any of it well. He was upset and really pissed. We didn't exactly part on good terms, and I left without some things because…"

"Because, why?"

"Honestly, because I didn't feel comfortable there anymore. I had intended to be fully packed before I told him. I didn't have a bunch of stuff, really. I had moved in with him. But he found out that I'd quit my job when my boss saw him at a local BBQ place. He mentioned how he wasn't going to miss my gay ass, and he didn't know how Carter had put up with my ways as a roommate for so long. That's what I was to everyone, his roommate."

So much made sense now. No wonder Collin had reacted the way he did when he woke up and I wasn't in bed beside him. Hell, if I'd been shoved in the closet like a dirty secret, I'd probably act the same way. I sighed before I took Collin's hands and rubbed them in the ink and then put them on the fingerprint card. I missed the digital fingerprint machines we had in Denver, but really, this was the first time I'd ever had to fingerprint someone. Right as I finished, Jacob came busting into the office. He obviously wasn't out at Wild Creek yet.

"Cruz said there was an emergency. What's up?"

"I'll let Collin fill you in while I go put his prints and information in the system so we can rule him out. Also, I'm going to process the notes into evidence."

"What? What the hell is going on? What evidence? What prints?"

"Just rub your fingers together and the ink should disappear, Collin," I told him before I decided to go for broke and bent down and planted a surprise kiss on him. He opened his mouth immediately, and I swiped my tongue against his quickly before I pulled away and then left my office. Damn, I really was in trouble. The tingling he always made me feel was still there, and he may or may not even be interested in me. And now his crazy ex was stalking him. Fuck.

"What's going on?" Gavin asked as I walked by his desk again.

"Collin has a not-so-secret admirer. His ex is making a nuisance of himself and has started leaving little notes under his windshield wiper," I told Gavin as I held up the bag full of notes.

"Seriously? How does he know it's his ex?"

"Well, I guess he doesn't, really. But he said he thought he saw him a few times, and then this week the notes started showing up. He recognizes the handwriting as his ex's, so he assumed he actually did see the man and that he was the one leaving the notes. I'm going to submit them into evidence, and hopefully, Jacob will be opening an investigation."

"Damn. Nothing like this ever happens here. Well, Merry Christmas to us, huh?"

"Yeah. He said he had plans to fly to California tonight for the holiday. That doesn't help things."

"You going with him?"

"What? No. Why would I?"

"I don't know, Chief. Why wouldn't you?"

Collin — 11

"You're very distracted. What's going on, Collin?"

"Sorry, Daniel. I've just got a lot on my mind."

"You and your deputy make up yet?"

I groaned at the question, and my brothers and cousins laughed. I glared at Daniel and promised paybacks.

"Not really, no. End of subject, so just drop it," I said pointedly, and thankfully, Daniel did let it go. I'd been in almost constant contact with Dalton since I'd flown to California Friday night. Come to find out, while in college, Carter had gotten so drunk his blood alcohol level was over twice the legal limit. He was arrested for public intoxication while walking down the middle of the street and was fingerprinted when he was booked. His dad had gotten all charges dropped, but the fingerprints were still in the system. Luckily for me that was the case because the only other prints on the notes belonged to Carter.

He had to have lost it to be so careless. Dalton said that made it so much worse because if he felt he had nothing left to lose, he'd go to any lengths to get what he wanted or felt he deserved. That thought had kept me up since he'd told me two days ago.

"Collin!"

"What?"

"Dude! What's with you? Why didn't you just bring the guy with you?" Travis asked. I glared at my youngest cousin, but he laughed and threw a handful of popcorn at me. Optimus and Fritz were only too happy to clean it up.

"Collin, you're really distracted. What gives?"

"Sorry, guys. I've just got a lot on my mind right now."

"Well, maybe we can help. You never know."

"True. But for now, I'm not ready to share. I want to see how things go before I spill things. I don't want to jinx things, you know?" I told them, hopefully leading them to think that I was preoccupied with Dalton. And honestly, I was. He'd been on my mind nonstop since I said bye Friday night and went to the airport. I unblocked his number, and he glared at me. I actually felt bad about the entire situation. He was right though—I'd acted incredibly immature, and I'd be shocked if he actually gave me a second chance. Well, really, a third chance. I'd already blown the second one.

If I got another chance, there was no way I was going to blow it. I'd already decided that. And the unexpected kiss gave me a little hope. Maybe Dalton was willing to try again. Or just try—

we'd never really even got a start. Ugh. He was right. I was immature and an even bigger asshole than he was.

"Give up, guys. He's thinking about his guy. Collin, why don't you just go home? I mean, Christmas was yesterday. You were planning on going home on Friday anyway. Why not go home a day early?"

"I'm sorry. I—" My phone ringing cut me off. It was Dalton's ringtone, and if he was calling me this late, it was probably bad. "Excuse me," I said as I swiped to answer the call and quickly left the room. "Give me a sec, Dalton."

"Okay," Dalton told me as I walked through the house. I didn't stop until I was on the back deck, overlooking the bay. I was incredibly fortunate to have an uncle who was willing to take on four more boys beside his own four, and his house was the one I'd grown up in and still had plenty of room. More so now that several of us had moved away. "Is that the ocean I hear?"

"Yeah, probably. I came out to the back deck so I could have some privacy. It's almost midnight here, which means it's *after* midnight there. Either you're working the night shift or you got called in, which would be really bad if you're calling me."

"Wow. Say that again, only faster."

I laughed at the joke, but I knew bad news was coming. "How bad is it?"

"Well, you weren't overly attached to your truck, were you?"

"Shit. I guess not. Is it bad?"

"Collin, he set it on fire at the airport. It's a total loss. The fire department just left, and the truck was hauled in."

"How do you know it was mine?"

"I was able to run the tags because the bed of the truck is still somewhat less scorched."

"Shit. Okay. So I guess I'm going truck shopping. Dammit. Okay. I really don't need this right now," I told Dalton while pinching the bridge of my nose. I felt a headache coming on, and it had Carter Beaumont written all over it.

"Collin…"

"Fuck. There's more?"

"Yeah, baby. There is. When I realized it was your truck on fire, I called into the station. Gavin interrupted him while he was dousing your place with gasoline."

"What! Fuck! That's not my place! That's…shit! Okay, I'm going to grab a flight and head back. I'll let Jasper know, and maybe he can pick me up or something. Please don't tell me there's more. I can't handle more right now, Dalton."

"Only other thing is that he got away. Gavin started to chase him but stopped to call it in and put out a small fire that he started in the kitchen on his way out the back door. He's still out there somewhere."

I groaned and wanted to cry. Yes, I was thirty-two, but I seriously wanted to cry.

"Dalton…"

"I know, baby. I know. Let me know when your flight lands and I'll pick you up. I checked out the place, and he'd ransacked it. He was either looking for something, or he just wanted to be malicious."

"I didn't take anything of his, so it was the latter. Let me look into flights, and I'll call you back, all right?"

"Sounds good. When you get home, we need to talk, okay?"

"I figured as much. I'm not in trouble, am I?"

"Not unless you want to be, no. But we need to discuss some things about what's going on, okay?"

"Yeah, okay. Let me book a flight, and I'll call you back."

"I'll be up waiting."

"'Kay, bye." I hung up the phone and almost gave in to the desire to just bawl, but I didn't.

"That sounded serious. You want to tell me what's going on, son?"

"Shit. Uncle Rourke, you scared me."

"Sorry. But next time you want to be alone, make sure you are. Now, what happened to your truck, and what can I do to help?"

"I don't suppose you'd believe me if I told you nothing, would you?"

"No, I wouldn't. Remember, I raised eight boys. You can't get anything past me. Now, what happened?"

"So that was Dalton. He's one of the deputies in Crooked Bend. I've sort of been seeing him, and it sounds like we're definitely seeing each other now. Anyway, Carter followed me to Wyoming, and he's been causing some issues. Well, tonight he set my truck on fire at the airport. I guess after he did that, he went to my house and tried to do the same thing. I really need to get back to Wyoming and deal with all this."

"That's a lot. Do you think it's something they can handle? You know your brother and cousins are going to be pissed if you go back and don't tell them what's going on."

"Yeah, I get that. But that's the problem. I don't want them to get into trouble. He's not worth it. But anything the local law enforcement does, that's different."

"That's understandable. But you can't just leave and not tell them."

"I can. They know I'm distracted—"

"Collin, you can't leave and not tell them."

"Fine. But I need to call their boss first or something. I'm going to need him to tell them they can't go after Carter. Uncle Rourke, you know they'll try to go after him."

"Yes, they will. Okay, you call the airline, and I'll call Taylor and let him know the situation."

"Thanks, Uncle Rourke."

"That's what family's for, Collin. Now, go find a flight and get packed. We'll get you to the airport just as soon as we need to."

"Okay," I said as I walked back into the house and straight up the stairs to my old room. I got the number for the ticket counter and was able to get a flight that was departing just after five in the morning. I definitely wasn't getting any sleep tonight. I called Dalton back and let him know what the schedule was.

"That was fast."

"Yeah, well, I need to let you know my flight arrives around nine your time tomorrow morning."

"I'll be there waiting."

"That sounds bad. Are you sure I'm not in trouble?"

"No, you're not in trouble. But I'm not taking any chances until your ex is found. You can't go home right now anyway. Your place is a crime scene, and we have to call in a crew to clean up the gas in the house."

"Shit. Okay. I'll see if I can stay—"

"You're staying with me. And please don't argue. I don't want you staying with Jasper. What if he or Liam get hurt?"

"Oh, and it's better if you do? No, thank you."

"Collin, we're going to have this discussion when you get home and not until then. You're staying with me, period. We'll talk about this more when you get back. This isn't up for negotiation, Collin, so don't try."

"Who's asking?"

"What do you mean?"

"Well, am I staying with Deputy Andrews or am I staying—"

"You're staying with me, Collin. We'll talk about it tomorrow. Now go pack and get your ass to the airport. I'm not going to be able to sleep until you land, and I put eyes on you."

"There's more, isn't there?"

"We'll talk when you get here."

"Okay. Dalton?"

"Yeah?"

"Thanks for picking me up."

"I couldn't not pick you up even if I tried. I need to see you, Collin. The sooner the better."

"Okay. See you soon."

"Yep."

I looked at my phone, but Dalton had already hung up. Shit. This was bad. So very bad. There had to be more than Dalton had told me. I packed up my things and then went to tell my brothers and cousins. I already knew Daniel wasn't going to buy it. He could always tell when I wasn't telling the truth.

"Hey, guys. I need to talk to you," I said as I entered the room. They were all still vegged out on the sectionals as if they didn't have anything better to do. And honestly, they didn't. We were all on vacation for the holiday, and it was supposed to be a happy family time. I didn't want to be the one to ruin it.

"Don't lie. Something's going on because otherwise Taylor wouldn't tell us we'd lose our jobs if we left the state. So what gives?" Daniel grumbled. I could tell he was really pissed.

"Shit. Really?"

"Yeah, really. So spill," Jonathan said as he crossed his arms and glared.

I knew I wasn't going to get out of it, so I gave in and told them part of what was going on, and hoped like hell they accepted it as the whole story and let it go.

"Carter followed me to Wyoming, and I have to go back because he set my truck on fire while it was parked at the airport."

"What the actual fuck!" Daniel yelled, causing Optimus to growl. Yeah, he was completely in tune to his master's moods. Shit, this was so bad.

"Yeah. I have to go and fill out paperwork and all that fun stuff. And I'll need to get a new truck before next week." I pinched the bridge of my nose again. There was no way this headache was going to be held off. That meant flying was going to be really bad.

"Look, I knew you guys would be like this, and I appreciate it, but he's not worth you going to jail over."

"They'd have to find the body for us to go to jail," Jonathan said through gritted teeth.

"That right there. That's why I didn't want to tell you. Look, I love you all, but I have enough shit going on right now. Please don't add being worried about you three to it. Dalton is handling it. They'll catch him, and that'll hopefully be the end of it. I promise I'll keep everyone updated, but I really need you guys to promise me you won't do anything at all to jeopardize your jobs."

I looked at Daniel, Jonathan, and Travis, and I saw the moment when they somewhat caved. I could almost guarantee at least one of them wasn't going to listen and they'd end up in Wyoming and in jail. Or worse.

"Uncle Rourke, please."

"Don't worry, Collin. They want to keep their jobs, so they'll listen to Taylor."

That gave me a little bit of reassurance, but not much. Still, it was better than nothing. Now to just get back to Wyoming and figure out what exactly was going on and what was up with a certain deputy.

Dalton — 12

I was sleep deprived, but I wasn't going to be able to get any rest until Collin was back on the ground in Wyoming and I could see and touch him. I was done playing games, and I was tired of the dance we were doing. There were topics we needed to discuss, and things weren't going to be negotiable. Like Collin's living arrangements. Thankfully, and surprisingly, Jacob agreed with me on my suggestions.

I was sitting outside the Jackson airport, waiting for Collin's flight. One of the perks of being in my cruiser was that I wouldn't get told to move along, although I had gotten several interesting looks. Last I checked, Collin's flight was on time, so he should be out the door anytime. As if my internal thoughts of the man suddenly made him appear, he was walking out the door and directly toward me with a smile on his face. I quickly climbed out of my SUV, and then Collin was in my arms. He felt so good there, and I didn't want to let him go. I knew I needed to, but I needed a moment.

Pulling back from the hug, I gave his lips a quick peck, and then smiled with relief.

"What was that for?"

"I missed you, and I'm glad you're here and okay. Come on, let's get your luggage loaded. I have the day off, and we have a lot to talk about later, but right now, I need to get you home where I can just hold you for a bit."

"Dalton, what happened?"

"Not here, okay?"

Collin nodded and followed me to the back of the SUV. After we got his luggage in the back, we both got in the front, and then we were on our way.

"Who's a pretty girl? Huh? I missed you, girl."

I tried to not roll my eyes as my dog whined from between our seats at Collin's attention. Damn, why couldn't he miss me?

"What are you pouting about over there? The past month has been pure hell for me, and I've missed you like crazy, too."

"Really?"

"Yeah, asshole," Collin told me while smirking. Ah yes, there he was.

"All right, Backstreet. So, you need anything on the way to Sulfur Springs?"

"Nope, but you need to tell me what's in Sulfur Springs."

"My place. You're going to be staying with me for the foreseeable future."

"Oh, I am, am I? I was pretty sure on the phone I told you no. What makes you think you can decide for me?"

"It's not that simple, Collin. Jacob and I both agree that for right now, the safest place for you is with me. We're trying to find Carter, and so far, we're coming up empty. There's more to it though. Can you wait until we get back to my place, or do you want me to tell you on the way?"

"I'll wait. Honestly, I'm probably just as tired as you. I didn't sleep much last night and not at all on the plane. Can I take a nap at some point?"

"That's the plan. I've had very little sleep for a week, so the plan is to see to Daisy when we all get to my place and then crash, together."

"Together, huh? And you think that we're actually going to sleep?"

"Yeah, I do, because I honestly don't have the energy for anything else. As much as I'd love to spend all day with you, naked, I'm afraid I wouldn't be any good."

"Hmm, but naked sounds so good," Collin said as he gave me a heated look.

"I'm all for being naked with you. But just don't expect me to be able to do anything more than hold you. I'm exhausted, Collin.

Completely. There's a lot that's been going on, and now that I finally have you back here with me, I'm crashing, fast."

"Then let's get back to your place and I can take care of you. I haven't done much sleeping for the past month, Dalton. A nap will be nice."

We chatted about mundane things, ignoring the tension, both sexual as well as the result of the situation with Carter. Before long, thankfully, we were turning into my drive and then starting the long trek to my house. I hit the button to open the garage door once we were close enough. We both climbed out of the cruiser, and I let Daisy out and she took off to do her business and explore the yard. We had fresh snow, and I'd discovered that she loved to play in it.

"Do you need to take care of your horse? I'm sorry, I don't remember his name."

"It's Knight. And no, he's not here. I took him out to Wild Creek before Christmas, and I'm boarding him there for the time being. He seems to really enjoy having the extra space in the arena, and I've had a lot of weird hours lately."

"Yeah, I'm sorry about that."

"Don't be. It's not all you. Work has been busy, and not just your case."

"You sure?"

"Yeah," I replied as Daisy came running back to us. I grabbed one of Collin's bags, and he had the other, and after closing the liftgate of the SUV, we went into the house. I sat the bag down at the bottom of the stairs and went to the kitchen to make sure Daisy had fresh food and water. Once she was taken care of, I turned to escort Collin up the stairs, but he was nowhere to be found.

"Collin?"

"Up here," he said from upstairs somewhere. I checked the doors and windows and then climbed the stairs to the second level. I found Collin in my bedroom, just staring at the room.

"Something wrong?" I asked as I walked up behind him and wrapped my arms around his waist and rested my chin on his shoulder.

"No. I was just thinking that maybe I should have asked where I'd be sleeping instead of just assuming it'd be in here."

"Nope. In here's where I want you. Forget the fact that I don't have a spare bed in either of the bedrooms."

"Yeah, I saw that. They're empty. Why?"

"Well, the house is a three bedroom. I couldn't change that, but I also don't have a ton of extra furniture. I had a one-bedroom place in Cheyenne, and when I wasn't out on assignment with Knight, I spent all of my free time with him."

"I'm sorry you felt the need to board him."

"Don't be. Like I said, he seems happier there," I told him as I went to my nightstand and removed my gun belt. I put the belt in the drawer but my sidearm on top, just in case. "Listen, I desperately need a shower and will only be about five minutes. You're welcome to join me or wait until I'm finished. Or, you can use the shower in the hallway. Up to you." I turned and walked into the bathroom.

I pulled off my boots and tossed them back into the bedroom, but I put my uniform I'd been in for way too long into the hamper and then turned on the shower. I grabbed my toothbrush and brushed my teeth while I waited for the water to warm up. I did a double take when Collin walked into the bathroom, naked.

"You invited me. I'm not going to turn down an opportunity to get my hands on a naked, slippery, soapy you. Even if you're tired. I just need to be with you. I can't really explain it, okay?"

I spit out my mouthful of toothpaste froth so I could respond. "You don't have to. I get it. I feel the same way. And trust me, it's not that I don't want you, because I do. But right now, I really need sleep."

"And you'll get it, just as soon as we get you clean. But first, I think you need to take off your underwear and socks. The shower works better without them. Not that you don't look good. You do."

"Shit," I muttered as I leaned down to pull off my socks. Collin moved in behind me and pulled down my underwear. I felt a gentle kiss on the small of my back, and then Collin's arms were around me again, and his body pressed tightly behind mine.

"Come on, let's get you clean and into bed," Collin said into my ear before placing another quick kiss to my shoulder. Even with as exhausted as I was, my body was starting to take notice of our lack of clothing and close proximity.

"We'll think about doing something with that later. I'm sure that after we've both napped, it'll be much more enjoyable for us," Collin said as he pulled me into the shower. In under ten minutes, we were both clean and drying off. "Head into bed. I need to brush my teeth," Collin told me as he picked up a small bag I didn't see him bring in earlier. He set it on the counter and used the left sink to brush his own teeth. I left the bathroom with an odd feeling in my chest. Was it because I was overly tired, or because I really liked the look of Collin using the other half of my bathroom?

As I was climbing into my unmade bed that I hadn't seen in too long, Collin came into the room and climbed in behind me.

"Are we both sleeping on this side of the bed?" I asked.

"Nope," Collin replied as he straddled my hips and ran his fingers up my naked torso. I couldn't keep from moaning, it felt so good.

"Shit, that feels amazing." I looked up into the blue eyes of the man above me and lost a little more of my heart to him. What was it about Collin McKenzie that did it for me?

"Did you know that I absolutely love your chest hair? I don't understand why some men shave or wax theirs, but you, you have the perfect amount." Collin gave it a little tug, and my dick couldn't help but take notice. It'd been almost two months since we'd been together, and since then, we'd danced around each other, either trying to figure things out or ignoring each other.

"Collin," I groaned as I pushed my hips up into his, our cocks bumping. I gasped when Collin wrapped a hand around both of us and started stroking our cocks together.

"Dalton, I know you're tired, but you have to admit, we'll both sleep better if we take care of these first."

"Who said I was tired?" I asked as I grabbed Collin's arms and rolled us so that he was under me. I latched my mouth onto Collin's and mated my tongue with his. We moaned into each other's mouths at the same time, me from remembering just how good Collin felt in my arms the last time we were naked.

"I want you, Dalton. Please?"

"Yes," I said as I nibbled on his neck and down to his collarbone. When I tugged on his left nipple, he shoved his fingers into my hair and gave it a gentle tug.

"Stop teasing. Start fucking."

"What about foreplay?" I asked, looking up into his eyes.

"Fuck foreplay. Fuck me already."

"What if I want you to fuck me?" I asked as I leaned over into the nightstand and started rummaging around for the condoms and lube I'd bought after Jacob's wedding.

"Shit. You flip?"

"Yeah, for the right partner," I said, holding up the box and bottle. "Who's wearing the condom first?" Collin groaned and grabbed my dick and started stroking again.

"Don't make me choose. I can't think right now."

"Then in that case," I said as I pulled out a strip of condoms. I tore one off, opened it, and batted Collin's hand off my dick before rolling the condom down my own hard length. I needed to be inside Collin again, somehow staking my claim on him.

"This isn't going to be anything to write home about, baby. I need you too much," I said as I lubed up my dick, then lifted Collin's leg and circled his puckered flesh with my slick fingers.

"Oh shit. Minimal prep. I really need you again. It's been too long."

"No, I won't hurt you, baby," I told him as I slid in first one finger and then a second. When he winced a little when I added a third, I slowed down and raised an eyebrow at him.

"Don't look at me like that. I've had nobody since you. And before that, it'd been over two years."

"Shit, if you'd told me that—"

"You wouldn't have done half the things you did. Now, do some of them again, please?" Collin pleaded with me as he grabbed my biceps and pulled me down on top of him. "I want you." Collin's mouth met mine again, and after my tongue had battled with his for a bit, I pulled back enough that I could push his leg up and out again, giving me the room I needed. I lined my cock up with his prepped hole and gently started to push my way in.

We both groaned just as the head of my dick popped through the tight muscle. I stopped, both to give me a moment as well as Collin, but he had other ideas. "No, don't stop," Collin said as he grabbed my hips and pulled me into his body. I bottomed out and he fell back onto the bed as his channel clamped down on my cock.

"So good, Collin. I won't last. Stop squeezing me if you want this to go longer than a minute."

"Dammit, I'm good with a minute. The box was new. We can do this again later. But hell, I need you to do what you did last time. Please, Dalton, peg my prostate and make me come."

Collin — 13

I wasn't above begging, so that's what I did. I quite vividly remembered what Dalton had done to my body over and over the only time we'd ever been together, and I wanted a repeat. I wanted a do-over. I wanted another chance because, sex aside, I knew that Dalton was special. I knew that I could look for the rest of my life and I'd never find another quite like him.

Dalton pulled out of me and got up from the bed. "Did I do something wrong?"

"No, be right back. I'm too damn tired to change the sheets tonight," Dalton said as he disappeared into the bathroom. When he came back with a folded towel, I knew what it was for and smiled. I raised my hips when he nudged them, and then he rolled me onto my side and then thrust back into me.

"You ready or should I slow down? I meant it. I'm not going to last." Dalton slowed his strokes in and out of my body, causing me to moan and want more. I felt my toes tingle and knew it wouldn't take much more. I'd dreamed about him and gone without his touch for too long.

"I'm ready," I told him just before he grabbed my upper leg and wrapped his hands around it and thrust hard.

"Mmm, yes. More. Harder." Thankfully, my deputy obliged, and in no time, I was shooting onto the towel that was laid out under and in front of me.

"Damn, sorry, baby," Dalton said before he pushed in one last time, and I felt his cock pulse inside me multiple times. He wrapped his arms around my leg and held on when he started to fall over. After a few moments, he grabbed the condom at the base of his cock and gently pulled out of me before he knee-walked to the side of the bed. "Be back in a sec," Dalton told me as he grabbed the wrapper before disappearing back into the bathroom.

I really wanted to pass out but knew I needed to clean up, and it wasn't fair to Dalton to make him do all of the work, so I rolled over and grabbed the towel he'd thought to grab for us. I heard the water running in the bathroom before I got up too, and when I entered, I raised the towel in question.

"The towel hamper is over there," Dalton said as he pointed to a plastic hamper in the corner of the bathroom beside the shelf of clean towels. I added the messy one to it and then grabbed a washcloth to clean up. After we'd both cleaned up and made one last trip to the toilet, Dalton grabbed my hand and tugged me back to the bedroom and onto the bed.

"Shit, the light."

"Stay put, I'll get it," I said as I pushed down on his chest and climbed out of bed. I turned off the light, sending the room into darkness. He obviously had room-darkening curtains on his windows because the room was almost completely dark.

"Okay, that's a nice touch. But why the room-darkening curtains?"

"I have both curtains and blinds. I still work shift work every so often and need to be able to sleep during the day because I'm up all night. I can't sleep with the sun shining in my face, so I installed blinds and curtains. It helps. Helps with the heat and AC, too."

"I never thought of that." I pulled the blankets up over my body as I lay down, and I couldn't keep in my moan. Dalton's bed was heavenly.

"Yeah, I know. I like my mattress, too. It's one of the few things I splurged on. Unfortunately, I never seem to spend enough time in it. And until you, I'd never had anyone else in it with me."

"Really?"

"Yes, really. Take a nap. I'm about to pass out, and I need to talk to you later," Dalton said before breaking off with a big yawn. In no time, he was sound asleep beside me. I couldn't blame him. He'd said he'd been up for over twenty-four hours, and he hadn't slept well the past week. Hell, I hadn't slept good for well over a month.

I couldn't wait to talk to Dalton. Not only about the case and everything that Carter had been up to, but also about us. Because dammit, there was definitely going to be an us. Period. The man not only did things to my emotions, but I'd never had anyone that could make me lose my breath just by looking at me.

I curled up next to Dalton, and before I could think too much about it, I was fast asleep as well. I woke who knows when, and the bed beside me was once again empty. He and I were definitely going to have to talk about that.

As much as I wanted to stay curled up in Dalton's bed and roll around in his blankets because they smelled like him, I dragged myself out of it and grabbed some clothes. After I was completely dressed, I left the bedroom and went downstairs.

Daisy found me first at the bottom of the stairs.

"Where is he, girl? Huh? Where's Daddy?" She took off down a hallway and went into a room on the left. I followed and found Dalton sitting behind a desk. The room was bright, a big contrast from the bedroom and the hallway I'd just went down.

"Hey. Did you sleep well?" Dalton asked as he looked up from his laptop. A little unsure of what to do, I just stood in the doorway.

"Yeah. I did. Your bed is amazing. But you left."

"Sorry about that. I won't make a habit of leaving you in the bed asleep. Promise. But Daisy needed out, and I had a missed call from Jacob. Are you going to stand in the doorway, or are you going to come in?" Dalton got up and walked to the other side of the desk. It was then I realized he was wearing a pair of sweats with his T-shirt. And I'd gone and gotten completely dressed.

"Umm, I'm not sure. I just…"

"Come here, Collin." At Dalton's command, I did as he instructed and walked over to him. He sat on the edge of the desk and opened his legs for me to stand in between. When I was within touching distance, he wrapped his arms around my waist and pulled me to him. "We're going to have to talk, a lot. But first, you need to know something."

"What?" I asked as I placed my arms on his shoulders. I looked down into his blue eyes and couldn't help but smile.

"I want you here. I want to be with you, and I want to give whatever this thing is that we've got going a try. Understand?"

I deflated and buried my face in Dalton's neck. That was exactly what I wanted, and hearing it from Dalton was a huge relief. I gave his neck a little nibble before I pulled back and looked into his eyes again. "You don't know how relieved it makes me to hear you say that." I gave his lips a quick peck before I pulled farther back. My stomach growling let me know it hadn't been fed in quite some time.

"I was waiting for that. You interested in an early dinner?"

"Dinner? What time is it?"

Dalton looked over my shoulder before replying. "A little after four."

"Shit. That late? I bet I have a million missed calls and messages," I said as I pulled out of Dalton's arms and ran back up the stairs to grab my phone. I was supposed to call everyone and let them know I'd landed and what was up. I found my phone in the jeans I'd been wearing, and when I took it off airplane mode, sure enough, I had thirty missed messages and six missed calls. "Fuck," I said as I turned and walked right into Dalton's chest.

"What's wrong?"

"Oh, nothing really. I forgot to call my family and let them know I landed."

"Call and apologize?"

"Yep," I replied when I hit the green button on Daniel's contact. It went straight to voicemail, and my stomach dropped. "Shit," I said as I hung up. I tried Jonathan but got the same. "Fuck!"

"Okay, what's wrong?"

"They're all going to voicemail. That means they're probably on their way here. Which is bad. So very bad. I don't want my family involved in my mess. I don't want them to get in trouble. And them being here is going to be them getting in trouble." I tried Uncle Rourke, and he picked up on the second ring.

"You're too late. They'll probably be landing within the hour."

"How did they get here so fast?"

"They have access to James's jet, remember?"

"Fuck!"

"You should have called. Daniel is beside himself. He's really worried, and they're concerned that Carter got to you at the airport."

I groaned and buried my face in Dalton's neck again. He wrapped his arms around my waist and gave me a tight squeeze. "How do I stop them, Uncle Rourke? I don't want them to get into trouble."

"I don't think you can. Maybe you should talk to Jacob. I know he was talking to Taylor."

"Shit. That's not good. Thanks, Uncle Rourke."

"You okay, Collin?"

"Yeah. I just got distracted, and then I fell asleep. I'm good though. I'll call you later."

"I look forward to your call. Tell your brothers and my sons I said to check in, like always." I groaned at the mention of brothers. That meant Lucas was probably with them. That wasn't good.

"I will. Love you," I said before hanging up.

"Okay, we obviously need to talk, but I think I know what's going on with the call. Remember I said I had a missed call from Jacob?"

"Yeah." I looked at Dalton, and my heart sank at the look on his face. Ugh, that wasn't good.

"Let's go downstairs, all right?"

"I'm not going to like this, am I?"

"Well, I did say we needed to talk."

When we made it to the kitchen, I sat on the barstool that Dalton had indicated.

"Okay, so now what?"

"Now we talk while I fix dinner."

"Do you want help? I'm good in the kitchen."

"I'm sure you are. And we'll find out just how good, later. But no. Right now, I need you to sit there and I'll cook. What do you eat, Backstreet?"

"Really, asshole? We're back to that?" When Dalton turned and looked at me, I had an idea of exactly what he was doing, and it scared me because I was doing the same thing. Anything to lighten the situation even a little would help, but there was no denying it. I was scared. I got up and went over to him and closed the refrigerator. "I'll eat anything. I'm not allergic to anything that I know of, and I grew up with three brothers and four cousins in one house. All of us boys. My uncle is a saint, and we'll eat anything put in front of us. Anything you have to fix will be perfect. I'm happy with cereal if that's what you want. I often will eat half a box of Lucky Charms for dinner. It's just easier, and I often work late because I can." I couldn't help but look at Dalton with an intense longing I knew he could see.

"Damn, baby." Dalton cleared his throat, and I swallowed hard.

"Yeah. Okay, we'll come back to this. But I'll eat anything, so whatever is fine with me." I gave Dalton a quick kiss and then went back to the other side of the room. I needed to put some distance between us before I did something stupid. Like...nope, not going there.

"Okay, so baked chicken and maybe potatoes? That good?"

"Yeah, that's fine. I meant it, I'll eat anything."

I watched Dalton as he got out a pack of chicken breasts and a bag of potatoes. After everything was prepared and ready to go, Dalton placed both pans in the oven and then turned and looked at me from the other side of the island.

"So, Carter."

"Yeah, I've been waiting for this."

"I know. You know it was his prints on the notes. And he was seen on security footage setting your truck on fire. But what you don't know is that when Gavin caught him in your house, he'd stabbed all of your shirts right where they'd sit over your heart."

"All right. What else?" That was quite disturbing.

"Well, we found bodily fluids on the clothing as well as the bed."

"Bodily..."

"The same that you deposited on the towel earlier," Dalton said as he rubbed the back of his neck.

"Ewww. That's just—ewww. No. Really?"

"Yeah. Since he was caught dousing the house with gasoline, we figured he just didn't care or expect it to be found. But the house was ransacked. There wasn't anything he didn't break or destroy."

"Wait, are we talking a lot of bodily fluids? I mean, how much sperm does a guy have?"

"He had to have been there for a while. There was quite a bit."

"What else?"

"There's pictures of the two of you together. On them he'd written 'Until death do us part.'"

"He's lost his mind. Like seriously."

"I agree. Which is why you're here. It's also why you're not to go anywhere without Daisy, understand?" At her name, she came over to us and sat and whined beside Dalton. "That's right, girl. You're going to be Collin's shadow for the foreseeable future." Dalton leaned down and kissed her nose before he stood back up.

"What about you?"

"This isn't about me, Collin. It's about protecting you. Until we find Carter, your safety is a concern."

"I don't like this, Dalton. What about you? I don't want to put a target on you."

"There's already one on me. You're here, with me. I have no doubt that he doesn't know I picked you up at the airport. But this is my job."

I sighed but nodded in agreement. Arguing with Dalton would get me nowhere. Remembering something from earlier, I asked something I already knew the answer to. "What about Jacob and my family?"

Dalton — 14

"Yeah, that you're not going to like."

"Then that means exactly what I was afraid of. Jacob contacted Taylor and *borrowed* them, didn't he?"

"Basically."

"Fuck."

"They're better equipped to hunt down Carter. It's what they do."

"I know. But they're my *family*, Dalton. I don't want them getting hurt because of me."

"I understand that. I really do. But you have to trust them that they know what they're doing. They went after and found the guy who kidnapped Rhett. They didn't get hurt then. As of right now, we're not sure if Carter is armed or not. We know he at least has a knife, and it wouldn't be entirely impossible for him to get a rifle."

"He has a gun, Dalton. I lived with the guy for over a year. There were several handguns in the house."

"Were they his? He doesn't have anything registered."

"I don't know. He has them. He used to take them out to his family's place and shoot with them."

"All right, what exactly is it that your ex does? We couldn't find much of anything on him. But we're also small-time compared to bigger-city departments."

"Nothing remarkable. He's an accountant for his family's business."

"Really? An accountant?"

"What? Isaac is an accountant. Why are you knocking on accountants all of a sudden?"

"I just don't see you with one, that's all."

"Yeah, well, he was good in bed."

"Okay. That was something I didn't need to hear." I glared at Collin, a little hurt by his comment. When the hell had I become so easily possessive about someone? When I met Collin McKenzie, apparently.

"Okay, I'm sorry. I really am." Collin let out a deep breath and looked frustrated. "I didn't mean that the way it came out."

"Really? Then how did you mean it? Because how else could you have intended it?"

"Carter was good in bed. Not bad-looking. But that's about it. He's shallow and only out for what's best for him and what he wants. He might have been good in bed, but you're phenomenal. You do realize that you make me come without ever touching my cock, right? That's never happened before. Nobody has ever made me feel like you have, Dalton, and that scares me."

"Yeah, it scares me, too. I don't know what this is, but I want to find out," I said as I walked to the other side of the island and right up to Collin. I was going in for a kiss when "Baby One More Time" started playing on Collin's phone. I pulled away and raised an eyebrow in question, but Collin smirked and answered the call and immediately put it on speakerphone.

"Where the fuck have you been? Can't you send a text at least?"

"Hello to you, too, Danny boy."

"Don't fucking call me that! Collin, do you—"

"I'm sorry. I was exhausted and forgot to take my phone off of airplane mode. I'm with Dalton at his place." Collin buried his face in my chest and sighed.

"And where exactly *is* Dalton's place?"

"Like you don't already know that, Daniel. I'm fine. I take it you guys landed?"

"How'd you know?"

"Well, mostly because I know you. And when none of you answered your phones, I figured it out. That and my boyfriend here told me his boss called your boss and borrowed you."

"Boyfriend, huh?" I whispered into Collin's ear.

"Well, what else would you call us? You're more than a fuck buddy, Dalton."

"Collin, am I on speakerphone?" Daniel asked. I chuckled at his exasperated tone.

"Yep. Hi, Daniel. We've met once," I told the man, cutting into the conversation.

"Hey, Dalton. We'll be there in twenty. We need to speak with you guys."

"I'm sure we do. Better grab a bunch of pizzas before you leave Jackson though. I put exactly two chicken breasts in the oven, and I don't have more to add."

"Can do. Later."

Daniel was gone before I could say anything else. I looked at Collin in question.

"Pizza is always good. Ready to be overrun by my brothers and cousins?"

"Maybe. They can't stay here, you know. I only have the one bed, and I'm not really willing to share it with anyone but you. Hell, I don't even like Daisy in it."

"They'll probably stay somewhere else. I wouldn't think they'd want Carter to know they were here, would they?"

"I wouldn't think so, no. I'll let the chicken and potatoes finish, and then we can put them in the fridge after they cool. Maybe a midnight snack?"

"Sounds good. I'm really sorry."

"About what, baby?"

"About my family."

"Well, I already told you my boss called their boss. I really think I'm the one who should be apologizing."

"No, it's okay. Anyway, what are we going to do until they get here?" Collin asked with a smirk on his face. I knew exactly where his thoughts were, and mine followed, but we were again interrupted, this time by the doorbell. I groaned because I knew exactly who it was.

"Expecting someone?"

"Yes and no. I'm not surprised though," I said as I kissed Collin's forehead and then left to go let Jacob in. I wasn't at all surprised to see my boss on the other side of my door when I opened it.

"Hey. I hope I'm not intruding."

"Not nearly as much as Collin's family is about to. But it's all good. I understand. Come on in."

"Oh, hey, Jacob. I was going to call you. I have insurance. It should cover all damages to your house. I'm really sorry. I can't tell you how sorry."

"Collin, calm down. I have insurance, too. I don't know why you'd think I was upset with you. I'm not. You didn't do anything," Jacob told Collin.

"No? You sure? I'm the one that dated the asshole that tried to set your house on fire," Collin told my boss with a somewhat sad smile on his face.

"You had no way of knowing what he'd be like after you broke up with him," I said as I wrapped my arms around Collin's shoulders.

"True. He wasn't anything like this when we were dating though. I mean, nothing."

"Okay, that's something we should probably talk about. When I called Taylor and borrowed some guys, he said he was going to look into some things for me. I really don't want to know how he does it, because he's helped so much, but he's found some disturbing things on Carter. I'm sure your brothers have even more info. I know they've been in contact with him during the flight."

Collin groaned at Jacob's announcement, and I rubbed his shoulders to try and help relieve some tension.

"Do I want to know?"

"Probably not, no," Jacob said.

"Let's go into the den where we can sit. Should we wait for the rest of the guys? They said they were on their way."

"They've landed already?"

"Yeah. They called right before you showed up. They were grabbing pizzas, and then they were going to be on the way."

We walked into the den with Daisy following. She curled up on her bed beside the fireplace. Damn dog had beds in just about every room. Yeah, she was already spoiled. Once we were settled with me and Collin on the couch and Jacob in the recliner, the tension in the room seemed to climb.

"Collin, did you know about Carter's trust fund?"

"Trust fund? No. I knew he came from a well-off family. Old money. His grandmother was a complete bitch. His parents, they tolerated me. They thought I was struggling to pay my student loans. I guess they never stopped to think about the fact I made a good salary. I mean, I got a significant pay raise when I moved out here, but my pay in Alabama wasn't bad. I didn't need a roommate. If they thought about it, they would have known that."

"I think they did. Maybe on some level. Did you know his grandmother passed away about eighteen months ago and then his parents about six months ago?" Jacob asked.

"What? No. I haven't really given Carter or his family a second thought. When I left, I cut all ties. I wanted nothing to do with him. I was tired of being the dirty secret. I had an out; I took it."

"His grandmother passed from natural causes, his parents in a private plane crash. So now everything is Carter's. I guess he no longer has a reason to hide, and now he wants you back. That's my guess anyway."

"I don't want him back. I wasn't good enough to be introduced as his boyfriend when they were alive; I want nothing to do with him now."

"That's good to know," I said as I rubbed my hand up and down Collin's thigh. He looked at me and leaned in, wanting a kiss. I quickly cupped his cheek gently and gave him what he wanted. I knew exactly why, and I had no problems with showing affection in front of my boss. I was out, and I wasn't one to hide my relationships. Especially not with someone as amazing as Collin.

When we pulled apart, I smiled at Collin before I looked back at my boss, who had a goofy smile on his face. Yeah, I was probably a goner, but I didn't care. Collin was worth it, and I'd do anything for him. Sure, it was fast, but there was just something about him.

"So, what I believe is basically he feels like he's got nothing to lose. Which makes him dangerous."

"Oh, about that. Collin said he has handguns. But I know nothing hit when we searched the registry," I told Jacob, who got an uneasy look on his face.

"That makes things even worse. All right, I'll let everyone know. Collin, I'm sorry, but you're going to have to take some more time off of work. I'm concerned about him trying to grab you while out."

"I figured as much. I'll give Jasper and Sean a call. That is, if you haven't already done so."

"I did, but only because they work with you, and I wanted them to know to be on the lookout."

"No, it's all good. They all need to know what's going on. I don't want anything happening to anyone because of me. Dalton's already told me that I go nowhere without Daisy, so I'll have her with me."

"About that. She can stay with Dalton at the station when he's there," Jacob told us.

"Why? I know she's not really a trained guard dog, but she's pretty protective of Collin already," I told Jacob. I'd feel so much better if she was with him when he left the house. Especially if I couldn't be with him.

"All right. I'm comfortable with them, too," Collin told Jacob, who smiled at him.

"Yeah, I figured you would be."

"Someone fill me in, please?"

Collin looked at me and smiled. "I didn't know because he didn't say anything, but if Jacob says Daisy can stay with you, it's because Daniel brought his dogs with him. I'm right, right?" Collin asked, looking back at Jacob.

"That's what I was told, yeah. Is that going to be a problem with Daisy, do you think?"

"I don't think so. They get along really well with other dogs, usually. But once Daniel gives them a command, they become different dogs, and it's an amazing thing to see."

"Someone clue me in, please?" I asked looking back and forth between Collin and Jacob.

"Daniel came. And because he's here on assignment and I'm the assignment, he's not going to take any chances. He's brought Optimus and Fritz with him. They're his German shepherds. They are highly trained and will be super protective of me. That's what we're talking about. I didn't realize he was bringing his dogs, but I should have known."

"All right. So the house is going to have two extra dogs in it. Got it. I'm pretty sure Daisy will be okay with that." I nodded at Collin and looked back to Jacob to ask something but was interrupted by the timer on the oven buzzing. Time to pull the chicken out of the oven and wait for it to cool. "Be right back," I said as I got up to take care of our non-dinner.

Collin — 15

Don't get me wrong, I loved my family. I really did. But the thought of them being put in danger because of me, was upsetting. And, let's face it, I really just wanted to spend a few days alone with Dalton and try to sort us out. I assumed that was going to be difficult when there were going to constantly be people watching us. Mainly my family, but it wasn't.

They showed up with half a dozen pizzas, told us basically the same things that Jacob had already said, left Optimus and Fritz with me and threatened harm if I went anywhere without them, and then they were gone. Daniel gave me *the look*, so I knew he and I were going to be having a talk when this was all over.

Now, it seemed, that we waited. I'd spent two blissful weeks with Dalton at his place. He went to work on the days he was scheduled, and I worked from home or went back over to Knotty Springs to check in there. There'd been no more notes under the wiper of the truck, something I was thankful for since I was still driving Dalton's.

But we were still waiting, and nothing. So far, not a sign of Carter anywhere, and that was almost as troublesome and nerve-racking as the daily notes were.

"Backstreet, we've got to figure something else out. The guys haven't so much as seen a peep of Carter. We're doing something different."

"Well, I'm in a different vehicle, I have not one, but two dogs with me all the time, and I'm not at my house anymore."

"Yeah, but I'd think you moving in with me would just make him madder."

"Maybe. I'm not sure. Maybe he knows I haven't really moved in. I mean, all of my stuff is still at my place, right? Maybe he's in town somewhere. Maybe I should go back home? My place has been cleared, right? So really, there's no reason I can't go back home."

Dalton glared at me, and I found it a little comical. He looked really pissed.

"Are you about finished?"

"Umm, yeah?"

"You sure?"

"I think so. Unless there's something I'm missing."

"Do you really want to go home? You're not happy out here? With me?"

"That's not it, Dalton. We didn't exactly go about this the proper way. I mean, I'm only here because you and Jacob insisted it was the best place for me. That and the fact my place was a crime scene."

"Really? You think that's the only reason you're here? I'd thought we'd gotten further than that the past couple weeks."

"We have. But you have to admit, until all this happened, you couldn't stand me."

"That's not true at all." Dalton sighed and turned and left the den. I looked over at the dogs and then back at the hallway he'd disappeared down before quickly following.

"Dalton," I called out but stopped dead when I saw him staring at the back door which was wide open.

"Baby, I need you to stay glued to me and somehow get the dogs here to us," Dalton whispered. I quickly gave the whistle that would call the dogs and put them on alert, and they immediately came running. I walked up to Dalton and glued myself to his back and glanced around the place, wondering. "Do you have your phone?"

"Yeah," I said as I pulled it out of my pocket and handed it to Dalton, who typed out a message and then handed the phone back to me. I put it back in my pocket and turned to look behind me. Optimus, Fritz, and Daisy were on alert, and it was a little comfort, but not much. They'd be no match for Carter if he was armed with a gun. "Where's your sidearm?"

"Locked up. You know that."

"I do. But it's times like this I wished you had it."

"Me too. Come on, to the office." Dalton turned and we carefully and quietly walked down the hallway. He whispered to Optimus, then went into the office and within moments, came back out. The room was clear, so we could go in, and in we went. Dalton yanked me in, closed the door, and locked us in there with the dogs. He immediately went to his desk, and after opening the left drawer, he swiped his finger across the pad. The safe opened and he removed a handgun that looked nothing like the one he carried every day for work.

"Why does that one look different?"

"Because this is a Kimber 1911 TLE II. It's a .45 and is my personal sidearm. This one only takes one shot and he'll go down. And as soon as this is all over, you and I are going to be spending some time at the range teaching you proper weapons safety."

"I know weapons safety. Remember who my family is? I just don't know the difference between guns at a glance."

"Fine. We'll spend a little time going over all of the weapons in the house. But we're going to the range as well. I want to know you can handle a gun in case you need to."

"I can shoot, Dalton. Again, my family? Even though I—" I was cut off by Optimus and Fritz growling at the door. Dalton had me behind him and on the floor between the desk and the wall before I could even think, and then he was crouching beside me. If I wasn't so fuckin' scared, I'd think he was hot when in protective mode. But when it came down to it, it was just piss-your-pants scary.

When the dogs started whining at the door, Dalton looked at me with a raised eyebrow.

"Most likely, they've heard their master on the other side of the door. I guess we could crawl over and see."

"You stay put. I'll go."

"Hey, I'm going with you."

"No, you're not. Stay there. And if anything happens, get under the desk. I mean it, Collin. I…"

"I will. Promise." I nodded in understanding. There was a lot of shit going on, and it was all stacking against us. Fuck. Why him? Why now?

Dalton quickly moved over to the other side of the room, and after he heard something on the other side of the door, he unlocked the door with an audible click and quickly moved behind it. It cracked open, and then Daniel was there.

"The house is clear, you two," Daniel said as he walked into the room and went down on his knees and loved on the dogs, who were all whining and yelping, demanding attention from their master. Those dogs were my brother's babies, but I had no doubt they would attack if needed. It's what Daniel did. He was very good with animals.

"I know I locked the back door when I brought the dogs in."

"Yeah, it looks like it was opened from the inside. The upstairs window was open."

My blood ran cold at the thought of Carter being in Dalton's house. "Which window?"

"Your guys' bedroom. Jonathan is bagging the evidence for Jacob; he's on his way."

"Fuck." I bent over and tried to not throw up. Dalton's arm around me helped, as did Daisy's kisses. "Hey, girl. Thanks," I said as I gave her a quick hug before standing up and going into Dalton's waiting arms.

I laid my head on his shoulder and just breathed his scent in. The entire situation put me on edge, and I really didn't like the idea of Carter being in the house.

"Please tell me the asshole didn't jizz on our bed. I'd seriously be pissed if he did. We're quite fond of the bed, and the only ji—" I put my hand over Dalton's mouth to cut him off. I did not want my little brother to know about jizz on our bed or anything like that.

Daniel smiled and gave me a knowing smirk. Yeah, I was going to be hearing about this again. I was sure of it. Dammit.

"Well, from what we found, it's just a nice little note and a couple pictures. He's been a hell of a lot closer than we thought. I'd almost guarantee the pictures were taken with a telephoto lens, but he was still closer than we'd like."

"Okay, I've got the goodies, now we just need the sheriff. I'd give them to you, but since it's your house, we can't let you do that," Jonathan said as he entered the office. I was more than ready to get out of the small room. Four men and three dogs made the already tiny room even smaller.

"If the house is clear, why don't we go to the den? Collin would be more comfortable there," Dalton suggested. I was quite grateful for it and gave him a quick kiss but didn't step out of his embrace. I couldn't just yet. He seemed to understand and grabbed my hand, wrapped his behind his back, pulled me to him, and led me from the office. He was still in front of me, Jonathan in front of him, and Daniel bringing up the rear.

"Where are Lucas and Travis?" I asked, wondering about the other two.

"They're checking the perimeter and grounds with night vision equipment. They'll check in when they're finished," Jonathan told us as we sat down in the den. I didn't feel safe though. There were too many windows, and as if he knew exactly what was bothering me, Dalton got up from the couch and went to the windows and closed all of the blinds and curtains.

"I realize they won't stop a bullet, but if nothing else, they'll offer a little bit of privacy."

"Thanks. I'm sorry I'm on edge. I can't believe he was in the house while we were. And without us or the dogs knowing."

"Yeah, I'm a little surprised the dogs didn't alert us," Dalton said as he looked over at Daniel and the dogs.

"They would have protected you. I promise. What were they doing?"

"All three were curled up on the rug in front of the fireplace," Dalton told him. "What I don't get is how he got down the stairs without us hearing him. Those things creak every time we go up or down them."

"We'll have to look into it. It's possible he left through the window as well."

"Then how did the back door get opened?" I asked. It didn't make any sense at all.

"You ever think about putting in an alarm system, and maybe some security cameras?" Jonathan asked.

"Why? I live in the middle of nowhere. Normally, there aren't any problems."

Jonathan and Daniel's phones both vibrated at the same time, and they checked them immediately.

"They're following a Jeep that's leaving the area at a high rate of speed. If they catch up, we'll hear more."

This wasn't good. None of it was. I was ready for this to all be over, so I could just live my life, peacefully, out here with Dalton. Shit. Where did that come from? No. This was his place. Not mine. I'd become entirely too comfortable out here over the past couple of weeks. I had to go back to my place in Crooked Bend.

"You feeling okay? You just tensed up again."

"Yeah, just thinking."

"Well, think about something else. I don't like it when you're this tense and I can't do anything about it."

I smiled at Dalton and reached over and stroked Daisy's head. I was going to miss her, too, when I had to go back home. Dammit. I knew better than to get attached. I'd only known Dalton for two and a half months. It was way too soon to be feeling everything I was.

"Shh, it'll all work out, promise."

"You don't know what I'm worried about," I said as I turned my head and looked into his crystal-blue eyes. They were such a contrast to his dark hair and tan complexion.

"I can almost guarantee that I'm thinking about the same things. We'll talk when we're alone."

When I looked back at the other two, Jonathan was looking at his phone. "Jacob is here. He'll be pulling up within a minute. He'll have to let you know if you can stay here tonight or not."

"If there's just a small amount of evidence on the bed, then it shouldn't be a problem. Not unless Collin wants to go somewhere else. But I really don't want to leave the house unattended."

"We'll get surveillance installed on the house tomorrow. We should've already done it, but I agreed with the others. We knew you two needed your privacy, and it was already going to be enough of an invasion knowing we were all out there and following you. We already set it up around the outer buildings, but we didn't on the house. I'm regretting that now."

"Jonathan, I want this over. How do we make it stop?"

"We don't, Collin. Not until we catch up with Carter. But I really think it's time for you to go back to work and stop hiding. The more you're out, the better our chances are of catching the guy."

"Absolutely not. I'm not going to let him put himself in danger like that," Dalton said as he glared at my cousin.

Dalton — 16

No way in hell was Collin going to put himself in danger by using himself as bait. Nope, wasn't happening. There had to be another way.

I got up and went to answer the doorbell knowing it was Jacob. When I arrived at the door. I didn't expect to see Jacob and Gavin both there.

"Hey, Dalton. I heard you had a little visitor. Can we come in?"

"Of course." I stepped back and let them in out of the cold. They followed me to the den where a very anxious Collin waited for us. I went to him and wrapped him back up in my arms. As long as there was a breath in my body, I'd do everything I could to not let anything happen to him.

"Hello, Collin. How you doing?" Jacob asked.

"I've been better. Jacob, I'm tired of this. I want my life back."

"I know you do. We're working on it." Jacob smiled at Collin before turning toward his cousin. "You have the evidence for us?"

"Yep. I left it upstairs. I'll take you up. There's something I wanted to talk to you about anyway," Jonathan said as he walked off toward the stairs. What could he possibly want to talk about? I thought there was only just a small amount of evidence. My confusion must have been on my face because Daniel chuckled before turning and glaring at Collin.

I know it hurt Collin that his brother was so upset with him about the entire situation. But honestly, it was in no way Collin's fault. Daniel knew, but for whatever reason, he seemed genuinely upset with Collin, and it bothered me.

"So, Daniel."

"Yeah?" he man replied while still loving on his dogs.

"Wanna tell me why you're being an asshole to your brother?" I clamped my hand down on Collin's mouth so he couldn't interrupt us. He'd just started to say something, but that wouldn't do. "He's done nothing wrong, and yet you're mad at him. He doesn't show it, but it hurts him."

Collin glared at me, but I didn't care. I removed my hand from his mouth and replaced it with my own mouth. When I swiped my tongue across his lips, he readily opened for me and then moaned when our tongues met. I wanted him to know that no matter who was around, I didn't care. He was mine, and I wasn't ashamed of it in the slightest.

"I'm not mad at him. I'm worried about him though. Especially since his ex managed to get into the house while both you and the dogs were here. If you'd kept it in your pants, maybe—"

"Stop right there, Daniel. Apologize," Collin growled at his younger brother while lacing his fingers through mine. I wanted to set him straight, but maybe I should let Collin do it. I looked at him and gave his hand a gentle squeeze before I looked over at Daniel, who had pink cheeks but was determined to stand his ground. "We were both in here, watching TV, and the dogs were asleep by the fire. Dalton didn't do anything wrong, and I don't appreciate your accusations. Now apologize." I watched the staring contest between the two and was proud of myself for not getting involved, and at Collin for getting Daniel to relent.

"I'm sorry, Dalton. I do apologize. I'm worried about my brother. Please forgive me."

I thought about saying nope and being an overall asshole, but I wanted to stay on Collin's good side, so I didn't. I nodded instead just as we were rejoined by Jacob, Gavin, and Jonathan. I stood up to join them because I really needed to talk to my boss.

"All right, Dalton. Effective immediately, your request for vacation is approved. You and Collin are more than welcome to head to that remote cabin you wanted to take him to. Enjoy your trip, and I'll see you in a week when you get back," Jacob said, which confused the hell out of me. I didn't ask for vacation. And who went to a remote cabin in the middle of winter, in Wyoming?

"What are you talking about?"

"Well, you had said you wanted to take Collin away. Here's your chance."

Collin's eyes got huge, and I did my best to calm him. "Baby, I don't know what he's talking about. I never said such a thing." That was definitely the wrong thing to say because the shock turned to pissed off.

"So you don't want to take me away for a romantic getaway?"

"Oh, now it's romantic," Daniel and Jonathan said in unison. I was certainly going to have to have a talk with them. Soon.

"I'm not going to win, no matter what I say, so I'm not saying anything. The evidence. You've collected it?" I asked, effectively changing the subject.

"Yes, we have. And that's why it's the perfect time for you two to go away on your trip."

"All right, what aren't you telling us?" I asked. Now I was just getting pissed. "And can we even go upstairs to pack?"

"I'm not going," Collin said, adamantly.

"Baby—"

"No. I'm not going anywhere except back to my place in Crooked Bend. I won't let him run you out of your own home.

This is ridiculous. I can't let him do this to you. He was here because of me."

"Collin, don't. I don't like where you're going with those thoughts," I pleaded with him and hoped like hell he wasn't about to do what I thought he was. I turned to the others in the room and noticed the shocked looks on Jonathan and Daniel's faces. "Give us a few," I said as I grabbed Collin's hand and pulled him up off the couch and with me into the office. I shut the door and then pinned him between me and it before covering his mouth with mine. He responded almost instantly, and that was reassuring.

"Baby, don't do this," I begged, breaking from the kiss.

"Don't do what? Kiss you? You kissed me. I was just returning the favor. Besides, I like kissing you."

"Don't leave me. I…Collin, I…I really have feelings for you. Serious feelings. Wanna-explore-this-more feelings. You know, the kind where you wake up next to each other every day for the rest—"

"I love you, Dalton. I don't want anything to happen to you because of me. It would gut me if he hurt you."

Fuck, I couldn't breathe, so I crashed my mouth back onto Collin's and wrapped my hands around his cheeks to touch as much of him as I could. What I really wanted to do was take him upstairs and spend all night slowly exploring his body and letting him do the same to me. I couldn't though. I had to remember the situation at hand, and so I pulled away from the kiss, reluctantly.

I placed my forehead on his and just breathed him in. I already knew I could spend a lifetime with him and it wouldn't be enough.

"Marry me."

"What?"

"I love you, too. Marry me. Marry me tomorrow and we'll go away for a honeymoon to a secluded cabin. Let me take you away from all of this."

"Dalton. You don't have to marry me to get me to go away with you."

"I know, but I want to. I know you're it for me. I don't have a ring, but we can get some tomorrow. I don't want you going back to your place; I want you here, with me. Forever. Always."

Collin pushed me back from him a little and looked at me intently. "You're serious, aren't you?"

"I've never said those words to anyone before. And I've never meant anything more. I love you. I want to marry you. And I see absolutely no reason to wait. Unless you don't want to marry me. I know it's fast. But I know what I want, and you're who I want."

"It's insane, but yes, I'll marry you."

I yanked him to me, wrapped him up in my arms, and then pulled him down to the floor with me. My home office was too small for a full-sized couch, but there was plenty of room on the floor for the two of us. My tongue dueled with his as we both fought for control, and I decided to give it up to him. I wasn't disappointed.

Collin left my mouth for my neck, just below my beard, and he already knew exactly which spot to zero in on that drove me crazy.

"As much as I'd love nothing more than to strip naked and ride you right now, we should probably get back out there and join the others, right?" Collin asked as he pushed up my shirt and swirled his tongue around my belly button. Already he knew how to render me speechless and make it difficult for me to think.

"Umm, maybe? What was the question?" I asked as Collin reached for the button on my jeans. I knew we needed to stop though, so I grabbed his hand.

"See, you know what the question was. Come on, we have packing to do. We'll have to go back to my place so I can grab any paperwork I'll need tomorrow."

"Okay. Can we go tomorrow? Maybe we can kick everyone out tonight and I can have you to myself."

"Mmm, that sounds nice. Let's go," Collin said as he pulled me up from the floor. The last thing I wanted to do was leave the office, but I agreed. Now wasn't the time or the place. After adjusting myself and watching Collin do the same, I left the office with him and returned to the den.

"Okay. You two get things sorted out?" Jacob asked.

"Yep," I replied, but Collin rolled his eyes.

"Yes, we did. We're going to go pack a bag and then head into Crooked Bend to spend the night."

"That's good. Lucas called. They lost their tail when he got to Jackson. He had too much of a lead on them, and they lost him somewhere in the city," Jonathan told us.

"That's okay. Maybe he'll show back up soon. Dalton asked me to marry him, and I said yes. We're getting hitched tomorrow, so maybe that'll do the trick."

"What?" everyone in the room shouted in unison, and then it was chaos. I looked over to Jacob for help, but he started laughing, and I knew I'd get no help from him. Gavin, ever the calm and reasonable one, let out a shrill whistle that quieted the room.

"All right. Now that I can hear, congratulations, you two," Gavin told us with a big smile on his face.

"Thank you," I replied to him as Collin wrapped an arm around my waist. "We're going to go upstairs and pack a bag, if that's okay?"

"Yeah, that's fine. We'll all wait down here," Jacob said while giving Collin's family the stink-eye. I wanted to marry my guy, but I didn't want to alienate his family in doing so. When we made it to the bedroom, the bed had been entirely stripped, and that led me to believe that there was more to the story than I'd been told.

"That's not a good thing, is it?" Collin asked, looking at the bed.

"It can mean a lot of different things. I'm really hoping that they pulled the bedding in order to collect all fibers and such. I'll ask Jacob when we get settled in town."

"Okay. Listen, just ignore my family. They're just trying to look out for me. You have to admit, I don't have a great track record with guys. Until you that is."

"I'm not upset. And we don't have to get married tomorrow. We can wait if you'd like."

"No. I want to. We'll go out to California, and you can meet the rest of the crazy when this is all over."

"You sure?" I asked as I pulled Collin into my arms again.

"Yep. I want to do this. You know, Carter never said he loved me, ever, but he asked me to marry him multiple times. I didn't even contemplate it with him. But with you, it was easy. You're just right, Dalton. And I really want to explore everything with you."

"We will. Just as soon as things are cleared up, we're going to explore life together. Starting with a proper honeymoon. For now, I'll take you away. If Carter follows, that's great. If not, we'll have time together."

"Sounds good. I can't wait."

"Me either, baby. Now, I need to pack. I know you don't have a lot here, but pack something of yours if you don't have it at your place that you can grab."

Collin nodded at me and then went to the nightstand, and after opening the top drawer, he pulled out the box of condoms and the lube.

"I'm not sure how many condoms are left at my place. But I don't want to run out tonight."

"Mmm, I like how you think, Backstreet."

Collin smirked at me before he tossed the box and bottle into my bag.

"Asshole."

"Yeah, but I'm your asshole, baby."

"That you are."

Collin — 17

My bed, different room. And if we were about to get married, I'd be moving out to Dalton's place. It wasn't in the plans, for sure, but I wasn't going to complain about the fact that the man I'd fallen in love with wanted to marry me. Today. We'd packed a small bag for Dalton and then gone to my place in Crooked Bend. I needed my own bag, and Jacob let us know that all we needed to get a marriage license was our driver's license. That was easy enough.

But this habit of waking up alone in my bed had to stop. Dalton had been so good about it since I'd been staying with him. But dammit, his side of the bed was empty, again. I pushed up onto my hands and knees to crawl out of the bed but stopped at the groan at the door.

"Damn, baby."

I looked over my shoulder and met Dalton's very heated gaze. He was taking in my naked form, and I felt at a disadvantage. "Hey, where were you?"

"You remember our daughter, right? Well, she put her very wet, very cold nose right on my back to let me know she had to pee. I've been watching her take care of business in the backyard."

"Shit."

"Yeah, she did that, too."

I fell when I started laughing at that. When I was able to breathe again, I sat up and looked at the man I was about to marry. "You know I don't like waking up alone."

"I know you don't. But you need to realize, I'm not ever going anywhere. I won't be far, promise."

"I get that. And I'm so much better about it. I was just thinking that the first time you were in my bed with me, you were gone when I woke up. That's all."

"True, I was. I had gone to brew coffee. Which, by the way, I've done this morning as well. But it's a little chilly in the house; you might want to put on some clothes first."

"You're right. I will. Unless I can convince my fiancé to come back to bed with me."

"I'd love to, but I think you should know that when I went downstairs, your brothers and cousins were in the living room."

I groaned at that. Of course they were. But I shouldn't complain. I loved my family. Dearly. And they were here to help me with Carter, and they deserved somewhere warm and out of the subzero temperatures.

"All right. Let me get dressed. Are we coming back here before we say *I do*, or is that what you're wearing?" I asked, looking at Dalton's dark jeans and button-down. "Wait, if my family is here, why didn't they let Daisy out this morning?" I asked as I stopped in the middle of the room on my way to the closet.

"She was in here with us."

"Oh. I guess I was so out of it last night. I'm sorry, Dalton."

"Don't be. But to answer your question, if you want me in something else, I can change. Just let me know what you want me to wear."

"Nope. You're absolutely perfect as is. This is you and I don't need to have a big wedding. That's who you are, and that's who I'm marrying." I gave Dalton a quick kiss before I turned and walked to the closet to grab some clothes. Dalton stood in the doorway, leaning against the frame, and watched me get dressed. I tossed him a pair of socks, grabbed a pair for myself, and went to the bed to sit and pull them on.

"You know, I'd almost say you needed a chair or bench or something, but there's one in the master bedroom at the ranch," Dalton said as he looked around my bedroom. He was right though. Although I did have a bench at the foot of the bed, it was missing, so it must have been a casualty of Carter's when he'd broken into the house.

"Yeah. Think we can get this stuff into one of the bedrooms out there?"

"The one on the left, next to the bathroom, sure. The one on the right, it's too small. I thought maybe we could turn it into an office for you though. It has a lot of good lighting with those three big windows, and your drafting table would fit on the wall between the two. And there's plenty of room for shelves and anything else you wanted to put in there. But it might be a little cramped with a king-sized bed and all of your furniture."

"Really? You'd let me set up an office at your place?"

"Collin, it's our place. Not mine. You're about to marry me, remember? I think it's pretty safe to say that it's *our* place."

After I finished lacing up my boots, I stood up and stood in front of Dalton, who was still in just his socks. "Where are your boots?"

"The other side of the bed."

I nodded before I pushed on his shoulders and then climbed on top of him. My deputy was sexy as fuck, and I was lucky he'd given me another chance after I'd fucked up not once, but twice.

"I love you, Dalton. I can't wait to be your husband." I gave him a quick kiss and then climbed off of him to go grab his boots. We were going to be heading out soon, and I still needed to pack a bag.

"Do you want anything for breakfast? I made coffee, but with your family downstairs, it's probably gone," Dalton asked.

"Most likely. But they'll brew more. Is there even still food here? I didn't keep much on hand, and I haven't been here for a few weeks."

"Yeah, about that. There are some canned goods. That's it. Everything else was thrown out when the cleaning crew came through. It just seemed the safer thing. I'm sorry about that."

"Don't be. So no food. What did you have in mind?"

"I called Son of a Biscuit. Hawke is working."

"Coffee cake and coffee, it is. Let's go."

"Now you're talking."

I grabbed Dalton's hand and laced our fingers together as I led him out of the bedroom. In no time, we were at the bottom of the stairs, and I made a beeline to the kitchen, already assuming there would be no coffee. Four grown men, two of my cousins and two of my brothers, could demolish a pot of coffee in no time. I stopped short when I entered the kitchen though, and Dalton plowed into my back, almost knocking me over.

"Dalton?"

"Yeah, baby?"

"You didn't tell me my *entire* family was here," I said through clenched teeth as I looked at my uncle, his four sons, and my three brothers. All standing around the kitchen, all drinking coffee.

"Yes, I did. I told you when I came down that your brothers and cousins were in the living room."

"Yeah, but you said brothers and cousins. You failed to mention *all* of my brothers and cousins. And my uncle."

"Well, you never asked either," Dalton replied as he wrapped his hands around my waist and rested his chin on my shoulder.

"Hey, everyone. What are you doing here?"

"Really, Collin? You have to ask that? Why do you think we're here?" my youngest brother, Brian, asked.

"I'm not sure. There's a lot going on right now. Where's your wife?"

"She's at home. She wasn't feeling well and couldn't get off work on such short notice. So, you're getting married, huh? Were you going to tell us?"

"I was. But like I said, a lot is going on."

"We're heading over to Son of a Biscuit for breakfast. If you all would like to join us, you're welcome," Dalton told my family. So far, they all seemed okay with him. I had to remember, half of them had already met him before today, and he'd already met the rest, although probably briefly, this morning when he'd came down to let Daisy out.

"I highly recommend it. Lucas and I have been eating there on a very regular basis. The have great coffee," Travis told everyone else.

"You're behaving, right?" I asked, a little worried. The last thing I wanted was for Logan to get pissed about Travis being around Rhett. After Rhett had been kidnapped, Travis was one of the team that had found him and was the first to administer first aid. Travis and Rhett had grown somewhat close while Rhett was recuperating in California, but I think Travis was more interested in Logan, who only had eyes for Rhett. And Logan did not care for Travis. At all.

"Yes. I haven't seen or talked to Rhett since he got married. I know he's only there on Tuesdays, and I simply avoid the place on that day."

"That's not exactly what I meant, but somewhat."

"Don't worry, Collin. I'm not interested in Rhett, or his husband. I only want him to have the peace he deserves. I hope that Logan is able to give that to him," Travis said before he turned and put his empty coffee cup in the dishwasher. I didn't even realize I had that many coffee mugs.

"Well, we're going out to breakfast. Either the bakery or the diner. There's no food here to speak of, so either join us, or we'll see you when we get back," Dalton told everyone as he handed me my coat and grabbed his.

"We'll go. But maybe the diner would be a better choice. It seems...bigger," Uncle Rourke said. I had a lot of explaining to do with him. I was sure the fact I hadn't told him the full story regarding Carter was the first issue. And now I was getting married, today. Yeah, I wasn't going to win any nephew of the year awards.

We all pulled on our coats, and after locking up behind us, we piled into various trucks and SUVs and headed across town to the diner. It was still fairly early, but the town was full of ranchers who got up before the sun, so it was possible we wouldn't be able to find somewhere to sit.

Luck was on our side though, and we were able to push together three tables so we could all sit and chat. Dalton and I filled in Uncle Rourke and the others about our plans.

"You really want to get married?"

"I do, Uncle Rourke. I'm thirty-two. I'm more than capable of knowing if I'm in love with someone or not. And Dalton gets me. He's a good man," I said as I laced my fingers with Dalton's again.

"I'm not saying you don't, Collin. It's just that at Christmas, you were still confused about your relationship status."

"Yes, my relationship status. Not about my feelings for him. I fell for Dalton a long time ago. I just kept screwing things up."

"No, you didn't. We've worked that out. Now, no more of that. Are you ready to go get our license? They'll be open by the time we get to Jackson."

"Sounds great. And Judge Wilson is available to marry us?" I asked. I hadn't called him, but I knew Jacob was going to.

"Yes. Jacob texted me this morning letting me know that Judge Wilson could marry us at eleven. So that leaves us plenty of time to get the license, the rings, and then get back over here to say 'I do.'"

I nodded in agreement, and after we all pitched in to pay our bill, we once again loaded up in the vehicles. Dalton and I were going shopping while everyone else was going back to the house. I was fairly simple and worked with my hands a lot, so I knew I didn't want a flashy ring. Dalton and I picked out matching titanium bands with a hammered finish. I liked the simplicity of them, and he liked the fact that I wasn't being super fussy.

"You're sure? We can get fancier rings if you want."

"No. I really love those. I live on a construction site most of the time. And when I'm not there, I'm either in the office drafting plans, meeting clients with those plans, or I'm at home asleep. I love that they're simple yet elegant."

"All right. If you're absolutely sure."

"I am."

Dalton nodded at me, and we paid for the rings, then headed to the courthouse basement to get our marriage license. That took only twenty minutes, and then we had that very important piece of paper in our hands, and we were headed back to Crooked Bend.

"I feel like I'm rushing you. And I know your uncle isn't too happy with me."

"He's fine. You're not rushing me. I want to marry you as much as you do me."

"I still feel like I am. That's all. Don't get me wrong, I'm happy and relieved you said yes," Dalton said as he glanced over at me before he pulled into the packed driveway. So much for a small, quiet wedding. Already there were more people than I envisioned. And that was counting only my own family.

"Well, looks like you're going to get a good-sized wedding after all, Backstreet."

"I was just thinking something similar. I thought we were having a small wedding? Why are they all here?"

"I'm not sure. But let's go in so you can pack, and we'll find out what everyone's plans are."

I leaned over the center console and gave Dalton a lingering kiss. I could do that. He was mine, and if I wanted to kiss him, I could, and he didn't shy away. That made me love him even more.

Dalton — 18

Our wedding was simple and sweet, even with so many people in attendance. Hell, Collin's family alone added eight people. Well, Jacob wasn't having any of the sneak-away-and-get-married-quietly stuff. Nope, we had over twenty people in attendance. That was more than enough for me.

I'd been a married man now for six whole days, and we still hadn't seen a peep of Carter. We took Daisy and went out to a cabin up in the Tetons, but still, nothing. If Carter was still around, he either didn't know where we were, or he was waiting. For what, I wasn't sure.

Deciding it was past time for my sleepyhead hubby to wake up, I dove under the covers and started kissing down his naked torso. When I got to his hips, I encountered exactly what I wanted: his cock that was well on its way to being hard. I heard a sleepy moan from above when I licked up his shaft. That's what I was going for. When the covers were suddenly thrown off me, I looked up Collin's body with a mischievous smile on my face before I went back to licking my morning treat.

"Good morning, hubby," I said just before I swallowed down Collin's cock and sucked hard.

"Mmm, Dalton, more."

"I don't think so, baby. I'm in the mood for you to make me scream this morning," I told him after I pulled off of his already throbbing cock.

"Yes," Collin hissed out before I quickly found myself on my back. I loved it when he took charge and turned the tables on me. When he entered me, it was with slow, measured strokes that kept me right there but never fully sending me over the edge. Already, he knew exactly what I needed, and when, and was always willing to give it to me. When Collin started thrusting a little faster and a bit harder, I knew he was close. I went to start stroking my shaft, but then he started pegging my prostate, and it was over for me. I arched my back up off the bed while my dick released between our bodies. Collin thrust one last time and then held inside me while I felt him flood the condom with his own release.

"Love you, baby," I whispered before I turned and kissed Collin's ear.

"Love you, too. I so needed that."

"What's up? Why?"

"I don't know. I just have a bad feeling. I don't know. Maybe it's because we have to leave our cocoon today."

"Maybe. Are you concerned about going back to work? Or something else?"

"Honestly, everything. I really just want the situation with Carter to be over. I know they haven't found him. If they had, they—"

"Would have let us know. Yeah. I get it. Trust me. I want your ex out of our lives, too."

Collin reached down, grabbed the condom, and pulled out of me, reminding me that we needed to talk about not using them. As he held on to the condom and got up to go dispose of it, I joined him. We needed to shower before we headed home.

"Should we let Daisy out before we get in the shower?"

"Nope. She, like always, put her cold-ass nose on my back just as the sun was rising to let me know she needed to go out," I said as I stepped into the shower and under the steaming spray. I moaned at the feeling of the hot water washing over my body. I smiled when I felt Collin's hands closely followed by his lips on my shoulders. "Mmm, that feels good."

"I'm glad you approve," Collin said as he wrapped his arms around my neck and then kissed me. His tongue met mine in a now-familiar dance, and we ended up getting dirtier before we washed up and got out.

"I wanted to ask you something."

"You know you can always ask me anything, Dalton. I don't want anything between us. Ever."

"Yeah, and that's exactly it."

Collin smiled before he went to the nightstand and grabbed the box of condoms. "Want to ditch these now that we have these?" Collin asked as he held up first the box of condoms and then his left hand, and wiggled his finger that had his wedding ring on it.

"Yes. I've never…" I shook my head, not really sure how to explain all I was feeling.

"I haven't either. You're the first guy I've been with in two years. I've already told you my entire history. I've been tested, but I don't mind getting tested again."

I nodded at Collin, but I needed him to know I trusted him. "Baby, I trust you. With my life. If you want to get tested, we can. I'm tested every six months because of work, but we can go together."

"We can get tested together. I have nothing to hide, and never will, Dalton."

"Sounds good. The only things I'll ever keep from you will be because work requires it."

"I understand that," Collin said as he pulled on his clothes. We quickly dressed and stripped the bed as instructed. One of the good things about living in a touristy area is that there were timeshares that were almost always available at a moment's notice.

We packed up our stuff, cleaned out the few groceries we had left, let Daisy out to take care of business one last time, and then we were off.

"Hey, do you have a name for your ranch?" Collin asked on the drive back to Sulfur Springs.

"No. It's only just over fifty acres. Not really a ranch. As far as I know, it didn't have a name when I purchased it. I wasn't planning on naming it. I have a horse, a dog, and now a husband. If you ride, we can get another horse, but otherwise, I'm not really looking to add a bunch of animals. And the place isn't that big. Nothing like where Sean lives."

"No, Wild Creek is massive. I was just curious." Collin reached over and turned up the fan on the heater. He was obviously cold. I chuckled while glancing at him and then back at the road. We'd gotten a little snow, but nothing like the previous winter.

In no time, we were pulling back into the driveway that would lead us to our place. So much had happened so fast that I hadn't had time to take care of a lot of things. I needed to make an appointment with my lawyer ASAP to update everything. I didn't talk to my parents nearly enough for them to warrant getting anything if something should happen to me. Yes, I worked in a very small-town department, but when it came down to it, I still carried a sidearm and a badge on a daily basis.

"You've gone quiet. You okay?"

"What? Oh, yeah. Just thinking. I need to meet with my lawyer and get things updated."

"I asked Simon to update everything for me. He should have all of my documents ready for me when I go back to work on Monday."

"I guess I didn't realize he still practiced."

"He doesn't. He keeps his license active and current, but he really only takes care of the ranch's stuff. But because I work with his husband, he just sort of seemed to lump me in with them. I'm sure he'd take care of anything you had if you asked him."

"I'll look into it. My lawyer is in Cheyenne, and that's a drive. Although, most things can be faxed or sent overnight." When I pulled into the garage, we got out and followed Daisy, who took off running around the yard. The place seemed so quiet. Maybe a little too quiet. It was almost eerie.

After Daisy was finished reestablishing her territory, we unloaded the bag from the back seat and went inside. "We'll have to go get food, most—" Collin stopped midsentence, and I plowed into his back. If I didn't have decent reflexes, we'd both be on the floor.

"What's wrong?" I asked, looking first at Collin and then up into the room. I laughed so hard I couldn't stand and fell over, taking Collin with me.

"It's not funny. I'm going to kill them," Collin said as he glared at me and then back at the stuffed monkeys going at it. They had put strap-ons on them, and it was so funny I couldn't stop laughing.

"Really? So deep down, you're a teenage boy?"

"Come on, Backstreet. It's funny as fuck. And you have to admit, the timing is perfect. With all the stress we've been under, it's nice that someone has enough thought to try and make us laugh a little. And really, what have we been doing for the past week?"

I got a little twitch out of Collin's mouth, and he finally gave in and stopped fighting the smile that wanted to show.

"What are we going to do with them?"

I looked back over to the little present his brothers and cousins had left and drew a blank. "I'm not sure. We could put them in the spare bedroom on your bed once we bring it over."

"That's a thought. Should we leave them as is? I mean, it looks like they're having fun, right?"

"Baby, don't we have fun when we do that?" I asked and tried to not laugh again.

"Yeah, we do. Well, I know I do. You seem to."

I glared at Collin and then attacked. I was on top of him and tickling his ribs until he laughed and shouted uncle.

"You don't fight fair."

"Sure I do. I just weigh about twenty pounds more than you."

"Hmm, true. But I like it," Collin said in a husky tone.

"Baby, I'd love nothing more than to have fun with you. But we have things we need to get done. And unless your family stocked the fridge, we're going to need to make a run into Jackson for some serious groceries."

"Getting naked with you sounds so much better, but I agree. They might have grabbed a few things to last us a day or two, but not anything else. Let's get some laundry started, and then we can run into town and grab lunch before going shopping. Sound good?"

"Yes. I'm not really looking forward to going back to work tomorrow, but you know I have to, right?"

"Yes, I do. I'll spend the day getting caught up on everything I've missed. I'm so thankful that Sean was able to cover for me over at Knotty Springs."

We were interrupted by my phone ringing, and I groaned before answering it and pulling Collin up off the floor with me.

"Andrews," I said as I answered the phone. I didn't recognize the number, but that didn't mean anything.

"Dalton, we've got Carter," Jonathan told me.

"Where?"

"You won't believe me if I told you."

"Try me."

"He's in your jail cell."

Collin was looking at me, a nervous look on his face. I pulled him to me and gave his forehead a gentle kiss. This was entirely too easy. Something else had to be up.

"Jonathan, I don't trust it."

"I don't either. That's why you two need to stay put until we can get someone out there for protection detail. Who knows how long he's going to be in jail or what he's got planned. But his hotel room…it's bad; Daniel and I don't want Collin to freak out."

"Got it. We'll wait here and talk when whoever arrives gets here."

"Sounds good." Jonathan was gone before I could say anything else.

"What don't you trust?"

"I didn't get the full details, but Carter is in jail in Crooked Bend."

"How?"

"I didn't get that answer. But I've been told we were to stay put until a protection detail arrives."

"I don't like this, Dalton. Did he turn himself in? That's really not like Carter, so what happened?"

"I'm not sure, baby. We'll find out just as soon as someone arrives. Hopefully, they'll have answers for us." If Carter was in jail, that meant Jacob was at the station processing everything, or on the phones preparing everything that was going to need to be taken care of.

When the doorbell rang, I was never so happy to see Collin's brothers as I was then. He was overwhelmed, and it was starting to show. We settled in on the couches in the living room, and Daisy was happy to be on her comfortable bed in front of the fireplace.

"What can you tell us?" I asked, looking at the two brothers who looked almost nothing like my husband. Whereas Collin had blond hair and blue eyes, all three of his brothers were dark-haired with brown eyes.

"All we can tell you is that Jacob got a tip from the front desk employee where he'd been staying. He was causing noise issues last night, and when the employee went to warn him, he got a glimpse of the room, left, and called the cops. Jacob got a warrant, called us, and we assembled a team and went in and grabbed him. If you want specifics, you'll have to get them from your boss."

"I'm sure I don't want to know specifics. So where do we go from here?"

"Our IT guys are working on his laptop he had with him. Until we know a little more about things, we want you two to stick close to home. If you have to go out, we want you to make sure you're with someone," Daniel said. I could tell he was worried about his brother. Hell, I was worried about Collin. It sounded like his ex had really lost it.

"We can do that," Collin said as he squeezed my hand. I quickly squeezed his back before I wrapped my arm around his shoulders and pulled him into my side.

Collin — 19

"Dalton, it's been two weeks. I have to go back to work. Not only is it not fair to Jasper and Sean, it's not fair to their husbands either. Carter's been in jail for two weeks now—if something was going to happen, wouldn't it have by now?" I asked as I buttered toast for breakfast before Dalton went to work. We were out of Lucky Charms because I'd eaten them all, again.

"Baby, I know you're restless, but I'm still not sure I trust your ex."

"You should never trust Carter. What aren't you telling me?"

"There was a large deposit transferred to an unknown account. Just as soon as we track it down, you're free."

"I'm sorry but I just can't. I have to go to Knotty Springs. It's my project and I've not been on site since before Christmas. I'll take Daisy with me. Or if you want, I can have Daniel bring Optimus back. Or Fritz."

"No, leave your family alone. They need time to relax."

"Yes. And I've had too much time sitting here doing nothing. I love you, but I won't keep hiding. I need to go to work. I'm sorry, but that's the way it has to be."

I could tell he was relenting. I wasn't going to give. I needed to go to work. I was going crazy cooped up in the house.

"Fine. But take Daisy with you and make sure you're inside the building, got it? And don't park super far away. I don't trust the situation at all."

I smiled at my new husband and gave him a quick kiss. That was still sinking in a bit. I was married. And I knew Dalton loved me and didn't want anything to happen to me—neither did I, but dammit, I was a grown-ass man and I had things to do.

"You make it sound like I was asking permission. I wasn't. You went back to work two weeks ago. I should be allowed the same."

"You're right. I'm sorry, Collin. We just don't really know what his endgame is."

"I understand. I really do. But I refuse to let him control my life, and that's exactly what he's been doing by my staying cooped up in the house. I need to do my job and go shopping, just as you have."

"I'm sorry. You're right," Dalton said as he wrapped his arms around me from behind. "Is that toast for me?"

"I'll share it and drop more. We need to get a bigger toaster now that there are two of us," I told Dalton as I handed over two pieces of toast for him. He promptly put them on a plate and slathered them with peanut butter. I laughed as I watched him groan when I pulled out the apple butter from the fridge.

"You didn't tell me we had apple butter. When did we get that?"

"I found it in the back of the pantry. Give that to Daisy, and you can have these slices. I know you have to get to work."

Dalton promptly tossed his peanut-butter-covered toast to our drooling daughter and then grabbed me and dipped me backward while kissing me. I was laughing so hard, the kiss was all but useless, but it was fun anyway. "You're amazing, you know that?"

"Why? Because I gave you my toast?"

"No. Because you truly are. You've been great during this entire mess, and I can't tell you how much I appreciate that. I don't want anything to happen to you."

"Well that's good because I don't either." I grabbed a travel mug and filled it full of steaming hot coffee for Dalton and handed it to him.

"I hate leaving you. Call me if you have any problems or if things seem off, okay?"

"I will. Promise." I kissed Dalton, this time without laughing, and then he was pulling on his coat and grabbing his Stetson. Damn, how did I get so lucky?

"Don't look at me that way. It makes me want to stay here with you and drag you back to bed."

"I wouldn't complain about that. Lunch? Wanna meet in town for lunch today?" I asked, hoping like hell he did. I loved the fact that when we were in town together, he held my hand. Call it juvenile if you will, but the fact that Dalton was proud to be my husband turned me on. All the time.

"Lunch sounds great. Does one work? I have a meeting at noon."

"It's not a lunch meeting?"

"No. Jacob and I are meeting with the mayor. We need to complain, again, about our lack of deputies. Christian has eight in his department, but we only have six, counting the two new guys. We need a few more."

"Okay, one. At the diner?"

"That works. I'll be there waiting." Dalton gave me another quick kiss, and then he was out the door that led to the garage. I heard the door rumble as it opened, and then his truck started. I looked down at Daisy, who was drooling all over the place.

"No. You already got Daddy's toast. You're not getting mine, too," I told her as I took a bite. Of course, seconds later, I was feeding her yet another piece, one I hadn't yet put apple butter on. Once the toast was gone, I poured my own travel mug of coffee, cleaned up the mess from breakfast, and put everything in the dishwasher. I pulled on my own coat, grabbed my bag with everything I needed, and then turned to look at a very confused Daisy. She'd gotten used to staying home, I guess.

"Come on, girl. Let's go bye-bye." That was all it took, and Daisy was charging toward me. I pushed the button on the garage door to open it, and she took off outside. After I tossed my bag in the front seat, I went outside to watch her squat. Once she'd emptied her bladder, she trotted back over to me and sat. "Good, girl. Let's go," I said as I walked over and opened the back door for her. I clipped her into her harness quick enough, and then I was in the front of Dalton's truck. We still really needed to get me my own.

In almost no time, I was pulling up to the jobsite at Knotty Springs, I grabbed my bag and then opened the back door to let Daisy out. I unclipped her, and then she was on the ground and trotting over to say hi to Denver, who had come out of the building.

"So you decided to finally come back to work, I see."

"Denver, I'm really not in the mood for your shit. I've had a lot going on, and if you have a problem with my absence, take it up with my partners. I know for a fact that Jasper was out here multiple times." I walked right past him and into the stone building. I needed to find my foreman, Paul, and get updates. Unfortunately, Denver followed and was right on my heels. I swear, the man was almost glued to my ass all day. I spent the morning dealing with him following me around. I'd finally had enough and stopped abruptly, causing Denver to slam into my backside. Both of us went down onto the dusty floor, a mass of tangled arms and legs.

"Really, Denver? What's your deal? You act as if you're my long-lost puppy or something." I did my best to shove him off of my back; the man was heavy.

"What the hell is going on here?" a high-pitched shrill screeched out.

"Fuck," Denver said under his breath. Then he was gone, and I was able to turn and look at the source of the noise. The most out-of-place, high-maintenance woman I'd ever seen in my life was standing in the middle of our construction site.

"Out!" I shouted as I got up off the floor.

"You can't talk to me like that," the brunette said to me while trying to look down her nose at me.

"I can and I did. Out, now. You don't have a hard hat on, nor are you wearing safety boots. Out now, or my crew leaves immediately," I growled out while looking at Denver.

"Rebecka, out. You've been told you can't be here."

"I wanted to see our spa. But what I saw was you on top of another man. Disgusting," she said as she glared at the two of us.

"Lady, I don't know who you are, or who you think you are, but get out. Last warning. If you don't, I'll physically remove you. You're trespassing. Out. Now."

"Try it. I'll have you slapped with an assault charge so fast you can't breathe."

"When you call the sheriff's department, be sure to ask for Chief Deputy Andrews and tell him it was his husband that assaulted you," I said as I advanced on her. She screeched, and then Denver was ushering her outside. Yeah, now so many more things made sense with Denver and his brother Hawke. No wonder the younger man had ended up moving out and all but refused to talk about his brother.

I was fuming and ready to break Denver's nose by the time he came back in. "Her spa? Really? Is she the reason why you're doing this?"

"No. I can't compete with the larger outfits around here, and if I don't come up with something, I'll lose Knotty Springs. Hawke reminded me about all of the hot springs we have on the property. That's where the idea came from."

"But yet you let her— "

"I know. And I miss Hawke every day. More than you'll ever know."

Something suddenly clicked, and I didn't know why I hadn't seen it before. "Denver, exactly how old are you?"

"Yeah, figured that out, have you?"

"Actually, just now. I didn't at first, but then Hawke's hair started falling out, and he stopped bleaching it. He's the spitting image of you. Which isn't usual for brothers. Hell, have you seen my three brothers? But anyway, it's more the age difference. Does Hawke know you're his dad and not his brother?"

"No, he still thinks my parents had him really late in life. I was only seventeen when he was born. It was a stupid thing, really. We were fooling around, and one thing led to another, and the next thing I know, she tells me she's pregnant. Her parents wanted her to get rid of the baby, but she refused. Then she died in childbirth. Too young and too many complications. Her parents blamed me, and I took the baby and ran because they threatened to keep him from me and make him pay for taking their daughter away." Denver flopped down on a pile of lumber and hung his head. Shit. When had he ever told anyone all of that?

"Fuck, Denver. Ran where? Where are your parents? Do they know where you two are?"

"Yeah. They did. They actually helped me run with Hawke. We settled here. It killed me every time he called my dad Dad instead of me. But it was the way they said it needed to be, and I was too young to know better at the time."

"Shit. You have to tell him. Denver, your son's gay, and your girlfriend has a problem with that. That's not cool, man."

"Yeah, I know. Do you know that Rebecka is the first woman to actually give me a second glance since I lost Susi?"

"Denver, man, you're selling yourself short. And Hawke's amazing. You need to fix things with him before you worry about getting your dick taken care of. Besides, there are some pretty amazing sex toys out there. I should know. Well, I've got Dalton now," I told the other man with a chuckle. "So Hawke's what, twenty?"

"He'll be twenty soon. His birthday is in April. He turned eighteen a month before graduating. He won't talk to me, Collin."

"I don't blame him. You chose a piece of ass over your own son."

"That wasn't my intention. I didn't realize she was like that. He never said a word, and then he moved out. I didn't know she was being so hateful to him until just recently."

"Well, it's Thursday. He's working at the bakery today. Why don't you swing by, say hi, and ask him out to lunch? But first, unless you're in love with her, you really need to ditch the girlfriend. I've heard stories about her."

"She lives with me now."

"So kick her out. Tell her it's not working and kick her out. You need to man up and fix your relationship with Hawke. That is, if you even want one. Not a day doesn't go by that I don't miss my parents. But I'm eternally grateful to my uncle Rourke that he stepped in and raised us when his sister and brother-in-law were killed. Give Hawke a chance. He's annoying as hell at times, but he has a huge heart."

"Yeah, all that damn sass." Denver shook his head and smiled. It was obvious he loved his son; he was just too damn deep in the deception, and he simply didn't know where to start.

"I'm meeting my husband for lunch. Stop following me around like a lost puppy, would you? Speaking of puppies, where's mine?"

"She's over there. One of the guys brought her a bone or something." I glanced at Denver, and he looked so sad. I felt bad for him. "Denver, I'm here if you ever want to talk. I'm not that close to Hawke, but I'm fond of the guy and he does talk to me so if you ever need an ear…" Denver nodded as I patted him on the shoulder before getting up.

I walked over to Daisy, and sure enough, she was gnawing away on a rawhide bone. "Come on, girl. Let's go meet Daddy for lunch."

When I said Daddy, Daisy whined, got up, and ran to the truck. After getting her buckled in, I headed to Crooked Bend and the station where Daisy would stay while we ate. I knew Dalton missed having her in his office with him. We had a lunch date with Dalton, and I was excited about it.

Dalton — 20

"You're sure that's what it is?" I asked my brother-in-law. Daniel had shown up shortly after I walked back in from my noon meeting. Which meant he'd been flying since before the sun was up.

"Yeah. The asshole wired money to a hit man. He's put a hit out on Collin. Uncle Rourke is going ballistic. He's with James and Taylor now. He's not happy, and I can't tell you how many times we've had to yell at him in the ops center. It's gotten so bad, we had to call Taylor and tell him to remove him. We can't hear each other because he won't be quiet. Taylor said James gave him a Xanax, and he's doing so much better."

"Shit. Fuck!" I left my office on the way to Jacob's but met him in the front commons area.

"Something can't be good. I heard you in my office, and I had the door closed because I was on the phone. What's up? Hey, Daniel. I didn't realize you were back in town."

"Five minutes. Give us five minutes with the asshole. Please," Daniel said from behind my shoulder.

"You know I can't do that. What's up?" Jacob looked from me to Daniel and then back to me.

"Carter put out a hit on Collin," Daniel told him.

"What? You're sure?" Jacob looked around and motioned us into his office. We quickly followed and sat down while he closed the door.

"How do you know Carter put a hit on Collin? You're absolutely sure?"

"Yeah. It was the odd wire transfer. It was most likely just a deposit for the job," Daniel told him. "IT found the account late last night. It belongs to a guy with a rap sheet a couple miles long. He's a known hit man and works mostly out toward Vegas. How he found him, we're not sure yet."

"Dalton, where's Collin?" Jacob asked. I didn't have a chance to talk to Jacob this morning since he came in late, and then we had a meeting. Work was hectic right now.

"He went to work. He said he needed to go to Knotty Springs because there were several things he needed to check on. Jasper had been covering for him, but it's his project. He called when he arrived. I haven't heard from him since, but I didn't expect to."

"What do you mean he went to work? Why isn't he safe at home?" Daniel growled through gritted teeth.

"Daniel, not now, please. Your brother is a grown man. He's been home from work for over a month now. He's tired of sitting at the house. And ultimately, I can't keep him locked up." I glanced at Daniel before I pulled out my phone and called my husband. When he didn't answer and the phone went to voicemail, I looked at Daniel and saw alarm. So, I tried texting him. Nothing.

"Okay, just give him a few and try again. Maybe they were running a saw or something and he didn't hear his phone ring," Jacob told me. It made sense. I'd been on that site with him before. It did get loud at times. Jacob cut into my thoughts though. "So what do you know?" he asked, looking directly at Daniel.

"About the hit man? Nothing favorable. He's ruthless and good. Which makes him great at his job, but that's bad for my brother. And we're not sure if the hit is on Collin, Dalton, or both. That's why I asked for a few minutes with Carter. I just need a couple minutes and I'll have the answers we need, Jacob," Daniel said while looking directly at Jacob.

"Daniel, you know I can't do that. I could lose my job if something like that happens. I happen to like my job and want to keep it," Jacob told him with an apologetic look.

"Wait, you said the hit was on Collin," I said, cutting into the conversation. I had only been half listening, but my interest was piqued now.

"We're not a hundred percent sure, Dalton. After analyzing the stuff from the hotel room, that combined with the funds wired to a known hit man, we believe a job was placed. First thoughts would be that he wanted you out of the picture, but Carter doesn't seem rational. He views Collin as his. He wanted him back, but Collin moved on. So now we think that he'll see Collin as betraying him and want to inflict pain on him. We just don't know," Daniel told me.

"I can't let you see him. Even if I was willing to stretch the rules, I can't because he's not here," Jacob said to the two of us.

"When did that happen?" I asked. Carter had been in our little county jail for two weeks now.

"They moved him late last night. He's in lockup in Jackson. Their facility is bigger and has more security. He was supposed to have been moved last week, but we had that ice storm that came through, so they delayed it. I'm sorry, Daniel. I really am. It's completely out of my hands. If you'd read your interoffice memo, you'd have known that," Jacob said, looking first at Daniel and then at me.

"Shit. And you're sure he's there?" Daniel asked. I could hear the worry in his voice. I didn't blame him though; I felt the same way.

"I'm sure. I followed them the entire way there and watched them process him in. Unless he's paid off someone on the inside, he's still there," Jacob told us, reassuring us.

I nodded at that and tried again to text Collin. He finally replied by calling back. I was so relieved to see his smiling face on my phone when his call came.

"Baby, where are you?"

"Sorry, Dalton, it's Paul. Collin must have dropped his phone when he and Denver ended up on the floor."

I pinched the bridge of my nose, not quite sure how to process that news. What the hell? "What do you mean, when they ended up on the floor?"

"Well, Denver followed Collin around all morning, annoying the hell out of him. He stopped all of a sudden for some reason, and Denver plowed into him from behind. They both went down on the floor with Denver on top of Collin. Then that she-cat came in and found them on the floor. She screeched and went on about shit, and then she was threatening Collin when he told her to get out and that she was trespassing. I mean, it's fuckin' January, man. Who the hell wears a skirt and heels in January to a construction site? It was comical and it wasn't. But shit, man, can this job be over yet?"

"Okay, Paul. Let Jasper or Sean know what happened. I know Jasper warned her several times over the past month. She knows she's not supposed to be out there. Do you know where Collin is?"

"He left with Daisy. I thought he said he was going to lunch with you."

"All right, thanks. Hold on to his phone for me, would ya?"

"Yeah, sure. I'll give it to him when he gets back from lunch."

"Thanks again, Paul." I hung up the phone and looked at Daniel and Jacob. "He's on his way here, and his phone is at the site. Paul said he must have dropped it when he and Denver fell. Long story and I know I only got a snippet of it," I told them when they both raised their eyebrows at that.

"What the hell. That's not like Collin," Daniel told us.

"No, it's not. Not from what I've learned about him. But did he tell you when he left?" Jacob asked.

"No. I forgot to ask. I'm going to head out that way and see if I can cut him off. I don't know what to do, Jacob. What does one do when their spouse has a hit out on them? Or maybe the both of us do?"

"I don't even need five minutes, Jacob, if I can get in to see Carter," Daniel said. I had no doubt whatsoever that it wouldn't take long for Daniel to get any information out of Collin's ex.

"Did you arrive alone?" Jacob questioned Daniel.

"You can't be serious. You really think only one of us would come knowing what we do? No, we're all here. You just can't see any of the others. Taylor knows how important this is to us. Those of us that aren't on assignment are here. He didn't call you?"

"He didn't call my cell, no. And I haven't yet had the chance to check my messages. I came in late and went directly into a meeting with the mayor. How many do I have on the top of buildings in my town right now?" Jacob asked.

"Well, Lucas and Jonathan are high. Travis is walking around town, as are a few other guys. We're all wired."

"Dammit. I need to know when shit like this is happening. Christian is pretty cool, but I don't want to have to fight him and his guys if a shootout starts. Any chance the guy we're after will mistake Travis for Collin? They look a lot alike."

"Not after what we did to his hair, no. We thought of that. We didn't want Travis to be an unintentional target either."

"Okay, so again, I'm going to go see if I can meet Collin outside of town or something. Who knows how long we have before this guy takes a shot. I just got my husband; I'm not ready to give him up just yet. I need at least fifty more years." At least that got a small smile out of Daniel.

I got up and left Jacob's office to head back to mine so I could grab my jacket and Stetson. After putting both on, I walked out of my office, closing the door behind me to run back into Jacob.

"Dalton, I understand, but you have no idea how, where, or when. What are you going to do? Keep him locked up like he has been?" Jacob asked.

"No, that wasn't fair to him at all. He understood and at first he didn't mind. But it got old, quick."

"Maybe you two could go—"

"Jacob, what would you do if it was Isaac? Hmm? What if it were *your* husband that was in danger?" I asked as I walked through the station and out the door with him following behind me. I had one thought on my mind, and that was find Collin and warn him. He needed to know what we were facing and to be on the lookout. We were outside on the sidewalk, still arguing when Collin pulled up in my truck. I was so thankful he'd made it to town without incident though. I watched as he climbed out of the driver's seat and then went to the back to let Daisy out. She jumped down and came running to me, but I was watching Collin. I reached down and patted her head, but I was focused on Collin. I needed to get him inside so I could warn him about what his family had discovered about his ex, so I started walking toward him.

"Get him down! Sniper!" Daniel shouted from the doorway, and I took off running at Collin. He was only about fifteen or so feet from me, but it felt like miles. The smile on his face faded, and I swear time stood still when I heard the too-familiar sound of the rifle. Several loud cracks came from somewhere, and then all I could feel was searing pain in my back and chest and I couldn't breathe. I stumbled before I toppled on top of Collin, both of us crashing down to the ground behind the truck. I fought for breath and then coughed, spewing blood all over the front of Collin.

I looked up into his face and into those beautiful blue eyes I loved.

"Love you, baby," I gasped out, but it caused another spasm and coughing fit. I vaguely heard more shots, but all I could see was Collin under me.

"Dalton! No!" Collin shouting was the last thing I remembered before I couldn't breathe and everything went dark.

Collin — 21

"Love you, too. Dalton? Dalton?" He was on top of me, and blood was bubbling out of his mouth and nose; it appeared that he was having difficulties breathing. All of a sudden, Jacob was on top of us, yelling, but I couldn't hear anything. All I could see was the blood coming out of Dalton's nose and mouth. Then he was gone. Jacob rolled him off me, and he was yelling into his phone, and then Daniel was there.

My brother picked me up like I was a rag doll, but I fought him when I realized he was taking me away from Dalton. No. I wasn't leaving my husband. When I turned back around, Travis was now somehow with Jacob, and they were talking and rolling him over onto his side. I saw the holes in the back of his coat and realized what they meant—he'd been shot. I lost it completely and collapsed.

"Noooo!" I shouted as I crawled to Dalton. I sat on my knees at his feet, hanging on as if somehow that would help. I felt Daniel behind me, but I was completely focused on Dalton. Daniel pulled me up under my armpits again, and I tried to fight again, until I noticed the ambulance in the street. I tried to listen to what was being said, but I could hardly hear. Everything was muffled, and I felt like my body weighed a ton.

"Collin, look at me. He's going into shock!" Daniel shouted right in front of me, but it sounded as if he was underwater. What was happening? Things started to darken and then…nothing.

I cringed when a bright light shone in my eye, and I shoved at whoever was causing the pain.

"Well, I see you're waking up. You're very lucky from what I've heard." I noticed we were moving and looked around and realized I was in the back seat of the truck. Who was shining the light in my eyes though? "He's awake and responsive, Daniel."

I sat up, or tried to, but the unknown guy pushed on my chest, keeping me on my back on the seat. "Dalton?"

"He's in the ambulance in front of us. You went into shock and passed out. I'm Donovan by the way. I work with the big lug in the front seat." I had to smile at that a bit. It was a good description of my brother. I tried to sit up again. This time it was allowed, and I saw that we were indeed following an ambulance. We slowed down and pulled into the hospital's parking lot; Daniel going to emergency room parking, the ambulance pulling up to the bay. I was ushered out of the truck and walked toward the ambulance. I saw Dalton on the stretcher, but he was rushed inside before I could catch up with him.

"Dalton?" I quietly asked as I looked at Daniel.

"I'll find out for you just as soon as I get you checked in."

"No. I'm fine."

"No, you're not. You *will* be seen. That's not negotiable, Collin. You're going to need to be as healthy as possible for Dalton. He's going to need you."

"Daniel. How bad?"

"I'm not sure. He took two rounds to the back. One at least hit a lung. I'll be sure to let them know you're married."

I nodded but otherwise didn't respond. I walked through the doors and was immediately ushered to the back. I looked around for Dalton but didn't see him anywhere.

"Dalton?" I asked the doctor as soon as he walked in the room.

"Nope. I'm Dr. Wall. I've been told you need to be looked at."

"No. I want to see my husband."

"I don't—"

"His husband is the GSW that was brought in just now," Daniel told Dr. Wall.

"Oh, I'm sorry. I don't know the status of him. I can find out for you really quick and be right back."

"That would probably make things easier in here," Daniel said before the doctor nodded and left.

"How you doing? You still feeling funny?"

"I can't lose him, Daniel. I love him so much. We just started our life together."

"Shh, I know. And I'm sure Dalton's going to be okay. Just as soon as we know how he—" Daniel stopped as the doctor came back into the room.

"Your husband is going directly to surgery. Just as soon as I check you out and make sure you don't need to be admitted, I'll have a nurse take you to the family waiting room."

"I'm fine. I need to see my husband."

"He's being prepped for surgery."

Daniel came to my side and sat down in a too-small chair and waited with me. I looked to him and reached for his hand. He grabbed mine and gave it a tight squeeze. "I'm sure he'll be okay. Let's get you checked out, and then we'll go to the waiting room and wait there. Jacob is around here somewhere. I know he'll find us and give us all the information he has."

The doctor looked between the two of us but started with my exam. I felt exhausted, but I was more worried about Dalton than anything. After the doctor went through all of his annoying tests, he deemed me okay but told me to take it easy. I glared at him and got up off the exam table. Never before was I so thankful that Daniel was there because my legs just didn't seem to want to work.

"I need Dalton, Daniel. I can't live without him."

"Come on. We'll go find Jacob. I remember where the OR waiting room is from when Rhett was in surgery. We'll go see if he's there."

I nodded to my brother and took the papers the doctor handed me and followed Daniel out of the exam room. We were met by Jacob just outside.

"He's in surgery. So far, that's all I have. There are two entry wounds, no exit. Now we just wait. I'm really sorry, Collin."

"I don't understand. I watched him put his vest on under his uniform shirt. If he was wearing his vest, how did this happen?"

"The shooter used high-velocity rounds. Our vests aren't perfect."

"Did they say how long he'll be in surgery?"

"Not as of yet, no. I wish I had more to tell you. I've been able to get some information out of them because he's my deputy, but you're his husband—you might be able to get more."

I nodded at Jacob and followed him when he turned and walked out of the ER and deeper into the hospital. After several twists and turns and an elevator ride up, we were finally at a quiet-looking desk.

"Hey, Sheriff. I bet you're wondering about your deputy."

"Hi. I am. But his husband here is wondering a little more. Can you tell us anything at all?"

"Oh! Let me get his things for you. We have them locked up in the back. You'll want to hold on to them. I'll page the head nurse, and she can fill you in on anything we know so far." The nurse behind the desk was gone before I could even say a word.

"The waiting room is just there. Let's go have a seat. I know you really don't want to, but right now, that's all we can do," Jacob said when I tried to argue. I knew there was nothing I could do but wait, so I might as well sit down before I fell down. The last thing I expected to see when I walked in the room was my family though, and it broke me. Completely.

Luckily, Daniel was still right there and helped me to a couch. I don't remember how long I spent crying, but I remember that no matter how hard I tried, I couldn't seem to stop. I didn't care that I was surrounded by men, my husband had been shot, right in front of me, and I was falling apart.

"Mr. Andrews?" I looked toward the sound of someone calling Dalton's name, but I realized she was referring to me. I didn't legally take Dalton's last name, but that was something to seriously discuss, later.

"Yes," I replied, wiping my face as best as I could.

"Hi, I'm Nurse Sumners. I have an update regarding your husband if you'd like."

"Yes, please," I said, trying to stand up, but Daniel and Lucas held me in place. When had Lucas arrived?

"Deputy Andrews is doing well. They've removed both bullets and vest fragments from his chest and have repaired his right lung. They're checking for additional injuries. We'll keep you updated as we get more information."

"Thank you."

"You're welcome. Sheriff McCoy, you're needed in the hallway."

I watched as Jacob got up and left the waiting room. Were all of these people here before?

"Collin, man, how about a clean shirt?" Travis asked. I remembered he was with Jacob and Dalton right after he got shot. I looked down at my shirt and realized it was covered with Dalton's blood. I rubbed the spots, but they'd dried, and it took everything I had to not lose it again. I looked to my brothers and cousins and a few others I didn't know, and I simply couldn't contain my grief.

"Why, Daniel? What did he ever do?"

"Nothing, bro, except love you and want to protect you. But we got the guy. Don't worry. He'll pay for what he did."

I raised my arms as Travis yanked on my shirt. Once it was off, he was pulling a clean shirt on. It wasn't mine, so it must have been a spare someone had in a bag somewhere. I watched as Travis balled the soiled shirt up and put it in a plastic bag that was at my feet. He reached in and handed me a wallet, a set of keys, a cell phone, and a ring before he sealed up the bag and took it across the room. I sat there, holding Dalton's things. His ring that matched mine I slid on my middle finger, right next to my own ring. When I touched the home button on his phone, the screen lit up to a picture of the two of us lying in bed and smiling one lazy morning while we were on our honeymoon.

"That's a good picture." I glanced at Lucas and smiled at my brother who was closest to me in age.

"We were on our honeymoon. Not that it was really planned. You know that. We were just so happy to be together. One of our favorite things to do is to be lazy on days off. We can't do it much because of Daisy. And when all this shit is over, we'll have Knight back to take care of."

"You're boarding him out at Wild Creek, right?"

"Yeah, for now. Dalton misses him though. Although, he's not going to be in any shape to take care of him anytime soon. Shit, where's Daisy?"

"She was at the station with the other guy."

"Which one? Seth?"

"He the skinny blond?"

"Yeah."

"Then yes. Isaac and Mack were going to come and pick her up and keep her for a few days for you. Sean had said he would, except he didn't know how their cats would handle having a strange dog in their territory. He also said they would be by later on, once work was finished."

I nodded at Daniel and went back to looking through the pictures on Dalton's phone. We'd only been married twenty days, but he'd somehow taken a ton of pictures of me, most without me even knowing.

After what felt like hours, a doctor finally came through the door. "Mr. Andrews, I'm Dr. Carter. I'm here to take you to see your husband. He's in recovery, but it's going to be several hours until he wakes up I'm afraid." It wasn't lost on me that the doctor's name was the same as the man who had caused all of the heartbreak. Carter Beaumont was the reason Dalton was even in the hospital.

"Go and see Dalton, and then come back when you need to. We'll be around. We won't leave you," Lucas said. I forced a smile for my family and got up on very uneasy legs and followed the gray-haired doctor.

We went through a set of restricted-access doors, and then he took me into another room, one that was cool, very dimly lit, and quiet except for the steady beep-beep of a monitor. When the doctor held back the curtain, I saw Dalton, the man I loved more than anything, lying there. My gasp was audible because the doctor immediately tried to reassure me.

"I promise, it looks so much worse than it is. He's doing very well for someone who just took two rounds to the back. The one bullet nicked his right lung, so we'll monitor that closely. He's on antibiotics and will be for a while. He's also going to be really sore because we had to crack his ribs. He has a chest tube, so be careful if you sit on his right side. We'll remove it when his lung clears up. You're welcome to sit with him for as long as you like. If you have any questions, just push the call button and someone will be in shortly."

"Thank you," I replied quietly. Once the doctor left, I walked over to Dalton's left side and sat down in the chair I pulled over. I carefully picked up his hand and laced our fingers together. His ring on my finger made me want to put it back where it belonged, but I knew I couldn't. Not yet. But soon.

"Please don't leave me. I need you so much, Dalton. You can be the world's biggest asshole, I don't care, but don't leave me. I love you so much. More than anyone. I love your sexy-as-sin smile and the way you make me tingle just by giving it to me. Fuck, baby, we just found each other. Please don't hate me. I'm so sorry he did this to you."

I couldn't help it; I laid my head down on the bed beside his shoulder and quietly cried. If Carter hadn't been after me, Dalton wouldn't have gotten hurt. I needed him too much to go on without him. I lay there crying for the pain I knew Dalton was going to face, yet comforted by the steady beep of the heart rate monitor. It was not quite the same, but it still reminded me of all of the mornings I'd lain on his chest, listening to the steady beat of his heart.

Dalton — 22

I was in hell. The pain was excruciating, and I couldn't breathe without there being more pain. I moaned, and then I heard a familiar voice.

"Shh, baby, don't move too much. I'll call the nurse," Collin told me. He was here, but why did I hurt so much? And why did my body feel like lead? I heard muffled talking, but it was too difficult to focus and comprehend the words they were saying. Collin was talking, but who was he talking to?

I cringed when a bright light was abruptly shined in my eye. I tried to pull away but stopped when I felt Collin's hands on me and heard his voice again. "Shh, Dalton, let the doctor look at you, please?"

I nodded, or at least I think I did. My head didn't want to work. But neither did the rest of my body. After more bright lights, more poking and prodding, and some immense pain, the doctor finally left me alone. I was much more awake, but my head was killing me, and it still hurt to breathe.

"What…" I stopped when it hurt to talk. What the hell happened? I turned my head slightly and moved my eyes so I could look at Collin, and my heart sank. He looked like hell. His hair was standing up and out everywhere, and he had dark circles under his eyes.

"You can have ice chips now and water later this afternoon. That should help with your throat. The nurse is bringing both as well as something for the pain. They started weaning you off of the good stuff a few days ago. I'd ask you how you feel, but I can imagine you hurt."

"Baby…"

"Shh. Don't try to talk just yet."

Collin looked at me, and I could tell he was barely keeping it together. When the nurse came in, she injected something into my IV and then was gone again. Collin came back into my line of sight holding a cup and spoon. I opened my mouth and moaned at the cold, hard, wet goodness he'd put in my mouth. Once those were gone, I opened up again and he obliged and spooned more chips into my waiting mouth. They were like little chunks of heaven on my tongue. Finally, I'd had my fill of them, and I kept my mouth closed when he tried to give me another spoonful.

"Had enough? Your pain meds should be kicking in soon, if they haven't already."

"They have. Hurts to breathe."

"That's what happens when you get shot in the lung. And the back. The one bullet was close to your spine, and I'm thankful it didn't hit it. The other nicked your right lung. They had to repair it. They said the vest slowed the bullets down immensely, and that's why they didn't go clean through you. If they had, they would have gone into me, and then we'd both be in here. Or worse."

"Baby, come here," I growled out. My throat was feeling so much better, but my voice still felt like I hadn't used it in a while. When Collin glanced at me, I saw the tears in his eyes that I had heard in his voice. He leaned in to me and laid his head on my shoulder and let go. I turned my head and gave him a gentle kiss on the top of his messy head because that was the extent of what I could do. "I love you. Let it all out, baby. I'm here." My throat started to protest, so I stopped talking and reached for him. I gasped when I did though. A sharp pain went through the right side of my chest when I tried to touch my husband.

"Don't move. You'll pull your stitches or your tube."

"Tube?"

"Yeah, you still have a drain tube in your lung. They were expecting it, but the infection you got was a little worse than anticipated, and you've been mostly out of it for a while."

"What day…"

"It's…I'm not sure. The days have all started to run together." Collin reached for the tray that was over me on the bed and grabbed a phone and looked at the screen. "It looks like it's February tenth. Why?"

I thought about it for a moment, my brain still sluggish. I'd been shot ten days ago. No wonder my baby looked like he did. "Have you been home?"

"You saying I smell bad?"

"No. Worried."

"I'm okay. Daniel's still around. He picks me up each afternoon and makes me go home for several hours and brings me back around ten at night."

"Get him?"

"Who? Daniel? I can call him."

"No. Shot."

"Oh, you mean the guy that shot you? Yes, they got him. Lucas got him. He sang like a canary, too. Not that it's going to help him. Carter isn't going to have any fun in jail either. He's too pretty."

I smiled at that. With all the pain he'd caused, maybe the man would finally get what he deserved.

"Dalton?"

"Hmm?"

"Don't ever do that again. If you pull a stunt like that again, I swear, I'll shoot you myself. I love you, asshole, and I don't want to live without you."

Collin was crying into my shoulder again, and it caused me to tear up. When I felt the tears running down my cheeks, I knew I should just give in as well. I couldn't yet hold him, but he was here, and he was safe, and that's all that mattered. Unsure how long we stayed like that, I fought the darkness as it came, but in the end, the pain meds won, and I succumbed to their pull and drifted back asleep.

The next time I woke, the lighting was completely different in the room, and when I looked to the window, it was dark out.

"He went home for a bit. Daniel made a deal with him, and he has to go home for several hours a day and try to sleep. They've snuck something to help him sleep tonight, so he might not be back. They figured it'd be more acceptable now that you seem to be more awake."

"Gavin?"

"Yeah?"

"Just checking. Water?"

"Yeah, you can have water. Here," Gavin said as he held a cup with a straw up to my lips. The water was cool and felt wonderful, and I greedily sucked as much of it down as I could, fearing he was going to take it away. "Hey now, take it easy. Nobody's going to take away your water, all right? The doc has cleared you for clear liquids now, so you can have all the water you want."

I nodded and slowed down. When the cup was empty, Gavin pulled it away for me. "More?"

"No. Thanks. I needed that."

"I imagine so. If you want something to eat, I can call the nurse. Maybe some broth? I think they said that's what you'd be allowed."

"No. I'm good. Tell me everything. How's Collin, really?"

"He's holding on. It's been touch and go, but he's got a great support system. You lucked out when you married into his family. They're amazing. He hasn't been left alone much except when he's been in here with you. Daniel and Lucas have been with him the whole time. They're tag teaming so he's always covered. The other brother, I can't remember his name, he was here for a bit with the uncle. They left and went back to California."

"Brian. His youngest brother is Brian."

"Yeah, him. He and his wife were here for a bit. Not long though. She seems…"

"Like a bitch? She is. She doesn't approve of Collin. Brian didn't know until after the wedding though."

"Well, that sucks. Anyway, they were here for a few days and left. The uncle stayed a little longer but had to get back to work. Speaking of work, you're going to be off for the next couple months. We got a new deputy. At least this one seems to know what the hell he's doing. The guy who shot you, he told where all the correspondence was between him and Carter. Carter's going down, big-time, if the DA can get the mentally unstable defense thrown out. Collin was the target. He figured if Collin would betray him, he didn't deserve to live."

"Betray?"

"Yeah, he broke up with him two years ago, and now he's married to you. Carter sees that as a betrayal."

I groaned at that. The guy was delusional. I hoped like hell the DA got the charges to stick.

"What about the shooter?"

"He was shot in the arm. He'll survive. They knew they needed him alive. So he's alive. He was released several days ago. He's in the pen over in Jackson awaiting trial. He had hoped for a lighter sentence if he ratted out Carter, but he forgot he had all of his correspondence together. His case has been turned over to the FBI."

"Wow. Okay. Good. I'm more worried about Collin."

"He'll be okay. You got a keeper there. Good for you. He loves you. Don't screw it up, or I might have to make a move on your guy."

I growled at Gavin, who laughed because he knew I couldn't do anything more than growl. "I thought you were straight."

"I am. But your hubby, he's got a beautiful soul."

"I know. I almost didn't give him another chance."

"You so were going to. That man had you so tied up you were walking around the station like a zombie."

"True."

"Do you want me to call and see if Collin is up? Maybe have him come back?"

"What time is it?"

"It's almost nine," Gavin told me after glancing at the wall. I turned my head and noticed the clock on the wall. Huh. I guess I needed to become better acquainted with my surroundings.

"No. Leave him. He looked terrible earlier. I want him to rest."

"He's worried about you. That man…you're his entire world, Dalton."

"He's mine. How's Daisy?"

"She's good. She's back with Collin out at your place. She stays there with whoever doesn't bring Collin here."

"Doctor?"

"Do you need to see him? Or the nurse? Are you in pain?"

"A little. Have questions."

"Yeah, let me call them for you."

Gavin stood up and reached inside the bedrail and pushed the red button on it. Good to know that the call button was so close. Within moments, the nurse was in the room, smiling at me.

"Well, you still look worse than that gorgeous husband of yours, but you're looking better. How you feeling?"

"Hurt."

"Yeah, I reckon you do. I'll get the doctor to order some more pain meds for you. You want some broth or more water?"

"No. Just hurt."

"Yeah? Where?"

"When I breathe."

"Well, a bullet in the lung will do that, but I'll send the doc in right away and have him look at ya," she said before she left.

"Good evening. I'm Dr. Jenkins. I'm the doctor on call this evening. How are you doing, Deputy Andrews?"

"Chest hurts when I breathe."

"Yeah, that's what the nurse said. Let's give your chest a listen and see what's up, shall we?"

I nodded and painfully made my way through his exam.

"Well, would you like the good news?"

"Yes. Could use it."

"Your lungs sound good. The pain is most likely from the drain tube. Since the drainage is almost nonexistent, I'm going to put in the order for it to be removed. It's been a while since you've had any pain meds, so the nurse will be in with those in just a bit. We're still going to put them in the IV for another day or two. We need to be sure your stomach can handle soft foods before we have you start swallowing pills. Once your drain tube is out, I'll have the catheter removed, and you'll be up and mobile."

"Is that a good thing? And that's why I don't have to pee, huh?"

"Yeah, well, you've been out of it for ten days now. It's mandatory for everyone getting surgery. It'll probably start bothering you more now as you become more coherent."

I nodded and watched as the doctor typed onto a tablet and then left. Moments later, a nurse arrived with a syringe.

"I hear you need some pain meds, huh?"

"Yes, ma'am."

"Where's that husband of yours tonight? He's usually here by now, isn't he?"

"Hopefully, at home asleep."

"Well, I can't blame him. But he seemed to sleep okay over on the love seat there, but I bet stretched out in a bed is better. I know it is for me. Just buzz if you need anything," she said as she dropped the syringe in the container on the wall and walked out of the room.

"What do you say? More water?"

"Yeah, that might be good. You're not staying, are you?"

"I don't have to. I can go out and flirt with the nurses. But I'm not scheduled to be anywhere but here with you this evening."

"Not working?"

"No, it's my day off."

"Just odd you being here."

"I understand that. Let me text Daniel and see what's up with Collin. You'd feel better with him here, I'm sure."

"No. Let him sleep."

"You're sure?"

I nodded and closed my eyes after pushing the straw away again. I swear, I hadn't been up long, but it didn't matter. I was so tired I could hardly keep my eyes open, so I gave in and let sleep claim me again.

Collin — 23

"Are you sure you're comfortable?"

"Yes, baby. I'm fine. Why don't you sit with me for a bit though?"

"Let me check the fire, and then I will."

"Collin, you checked the fire not ten minutes ago. What's wrong?"

"What do you mean? Nothing's wrong."

"Collin, baby, come sit down with me, then."

I looked over at my husband and relented. He was right though—I was stalling. I didn't want to hurt him, but I knew I might have trouble telling him no when it came to anything.

"Baby, what's going on? I know I already asked that, but you haven't answered."

"I'm still processing everything."

"Are you sure? You say that like you're unsure."

"Only because I might be. I'm so happy you're here and still alive, but dammit…" I broke and grabbed several tissues from the box on the coffee table.

"I'm sorry this has been so rough on you."

"You're kidding, right? I'm not the one who got shot. You are. And it's my fault. If it wasn't for me, you wouldn't have spent the last two weeks in the hospital." I wiped my eyes and blew my nose while looking at Dalton. His beard had gotten really thick while he was in the hospital, and he needed a haircut, but damn, he was still sexy.

"Hey, I guess I've been too busy looking at your eyes and smile or something, but am I ever going to get this back?" Dalton asked while touching the wedding band that was on my middle finger. Shit, I'd been so focused on him, I'd completely forgotten to put it back on him once he was feeling better. His stay in the hospital was up and down so much, I never knew if he was going to have a fever spike or not. He'd spent more time asleep than awake.

"Do you want it back?" I asked, looking down at the matching rings on my fingers.

"What the hell? Why wouldn't I? Do you not want to be married to me anymore?"

"What? Of course I do. But what if something like this happens again?"

"Got anymore crazy ex-boyfriends?"

"Maybe? I've had a few, but I don't think any of them are crazy."

"Well, if they are, I'd gladly get shot protecting you again. I love you. You're mine."

"I love you, too, Dalton."

"Good. Now give me my ring back," Dalton said, holding out his hand. I pulled the ring off my middle finger and slid it back onto his.

"Ahh, much better. Now, I'm not asking for sex, but dammit, you could kiss me, you know. I won't break. And I'm tired of those quick pecks you've been giving me for the past few days."

"I just don't want to hurt you."

"You won't. Now, can I get a kiss? Please? I even brushed my teeth for it and everything."

I laughed at Dalton pouting. He was adorable and I just couldn't. It was too much. I gave in though, like I knew I would, and scooted over to him, leaned in, and gave him the kiss he wanted. He kept it sweet, but when his tongue swiped across my lips, asking for entrance, I readily gave it and was thankful I did. I needed this as much as he seemed to. I needed to know he was here with me and he was okay.

"Baby, I'm okay," Dalton said as he broke the kiss.

"No, you're not. You now have two bullet holes in your back and a repaired lung. That's not okay."

"I could be dead, so I think I'm okay. Now, it's Valentine's Day, isn't it?"

"Shit, yes. I…"

"Don't worry. It's not like I've had a lot of time to go out and get you something. I promise to make it up to you when I'm a little more on my feet though."

"Are you kidding? You're here. With me. I think that's the perfect present. I'm the one who needs to apologize. I didn't plan anything."

"Why would you? We didn't even know I was going to be discharged until this morning. But as far as I'm concerned, this is a perfect evening. I'm here with you, we're cuddling on the couch, the fire is lit, it's snowing outside. What more could I ask for?"

"I don't know? Sex?"

Dalton chuckled a little but groaned when it pulled. I figured that'd be the case. He was hurting more than he was telling. "What makes you think I'm not going to ask for sex later?"

"You can ask all you want. The doctor already said no strenuous activity. That means no sex."

"No, that means no rough sex. But I'm hoping if I pout and beg enough, you'll give in and maybe suck me off?"

"Shit, Dalton, I'd love to. But you have to promise you'll just lie there. Understood?"

"Baby, you okay?" Dalton ran his fingers through my hair and cupped my cheek. I was close to losing it, and until this man, I'd never been this emotional before. But that's what happened when you found your person. They were it for you, and they had the ability to make you a complete mess.

"I'm trying to be. I feel terrible about what happened, and the weeks leading up to it didn't help. Then there was the hospital stay, and when you developed that infection, I swear, Dalton, that was probably just as scary as you getting shot right in front of me."

"I'm sorry, baby. I never wanted you to have to go through any of that."

"It's not your fault. There's nothing you could have done to prevent it, I don't believe. I'm just thankful you're here with me. I'm not ready to say goodbye." I ran my fingers through Dalton's scraggly beard and knew how I wanted to spend the rest of the evening. "Did you take your pain meds?"

"I did, yes. Why?"

"How about we retire upstairs? I want to pamper you."

"I'm never going to say no to being pampered by you. Lead the way, Backstreet."

"Mmm, there you are. I've missed you."

"I've missed you, too." Dalton gingerly got up off the couch and walked to the stairs and waited.

"Just let me check on the fire and make sure the screen is secure."

He nodded at me, and I quickly checked. I didn't want embers to pop out, but with the screen securely locked in place, it wouldn't be an issue at all. Once I made my way over to Dalton, he wrapped his arm around me and pulled me the rest of the way to him. It felt like heaven to be in his arms again. I needed this as much as he probably did, maybe more.

"Come on, let's go get you primped."

"Primped? I thought I was getting pampered. I was really hoping that entailed the two of us naked."

"Trust me, it will. Eventually. But first, you could use a trim."

"I could? Yeah, I definitely could. It's been a couple weeks."

"So we'll start there and then see where that leads us. But I promise, we'll end up naked at some point."

"I'm all for that. I've missed sleeping next to you."

"I've missed sleeping in our bed. Although, we're going to have to switch sides for a few weeks," I told him as we reached the top of the stairs.

"Yeah, I figured as much. I'll survive. I'm just looking forward to sleeping in my own bed again. And if you're on my left side, you'll get close, right?"

"Yes," I said as I directed Dalton into the bathroom. I had him lean against the counter and decided it was probably better if I trimmed his beard with his shirt off, so I started unbuttoning it.

"Hmm, I like where this is going."

I looked up into his eyes and sighed. Yeah, there was my guy. He was finally back home. Dalton ran a finger down the side of my face and stared at me as I finished unbuttoning his shirt and removed it.

"I love you, Collin. Don't forget that."

"I won't. I love you, too. Now, let's get you cleaned up so we can get you in bed. You said you took your pain meds, so you're going to get sleepy on me soon."

"I hate that about them."

"I know. But it helps. You need to sleep and relax so your body can heal." I grabbed the beard trimmer and turned it on. It buzzed to life and grinded away on Dalton's overgrown facial hair. Once that was trimmed up how I knew he liked it, I quickly undressed both of us and pulled him into the shower with me.

"Oh, that feels wonderful."

"Missed this, have you?"

"Yes. The shower at the hospital has a terrible showerhead, and it's like tiny little needles pegging your body. It was painful, so I only took the one shower."

"Well, we'll get you scrubbed clean, dried, and then tucked in."

"But I thought you said we'd…"

"We will, as long as you're still awake," I replied as I poured shampoo into my hand, then attacked Dalton's overly long hair. That wasn't something I was comfortable with trimming, so I'd take him into town in the next day or two to get it taken care of.

Once we were both squeaky clean, I turned off the water, grabbed a fluffy towel, and dried off Dalton. When I went down on my knees to dry his legs, I was faced with a plump dick that I hadn't had the pleasure of playing with for a couple weeks. Really, I shouldn't play with him at all, but I had caught the doctor in the hallway, and he assured me that as long as Dalton just lay there, a blow job or hand job was allowed. So that's what I had planned for my sexy husband. I gave his cock a quick kiss and then stood up to grab a dry towel for myself.

"Hey, that's it?" Dalton asked, pouting.

"Go brush your teeth. I have to dry off and clean up the hair off the floor."

Dalton nodded and carefully crossed the bathroom to the sinks and brushed his teeth. I made quick work of cleaning up the hair and tossing it, and then I brushed my own teeth before I went to the bedroom in search of my husband. I found him in bed, on the left side, fast asleep. I had to chuckle at that because he was adamant that he'd have plenty of energy for misbehaving, but there he was, fast asleep on my pillow. He looked so good there in our bed that I was afraid to join him for fear of waking him up.

I went to the dresser and grabbed a pair of sweats and a shirt and put them on before I quietly went downstairs to let Daisy out one last time. She took off like a greyhound after the rabbit when I opened the back door. I watched her play in the snow for a moment before I closed the cold weather out, filled her food bowl, and gave her fresh water. In no time, she was scratching at the back door, and when I peeked, sure enough there she was, so I let her in out of the cold.

"Now remember, girl. You have to wake me and not Daddy when you need out, okay? Let Daddy sleep and wake me. I'm on his side of the bed, so hopefully that helps." I gave her a quick dry with a towel from the laundry room and then checked the fireplace once again before checking all of the doors to be sure they were locked. It was a habit I didn't see us ever getting out of again. Once I was sure the alarm was set, an addition thanks to my family, I turned off the lights and climbed the stairs to the bedroom.

Dalton was in the same spot, but now he was quietly snoring. I knew he needed his pillow adjusted, and somehow I managed to do that without waking him, which meant he was most likely out for the night. It had been two long weeks since he'd slept here, and there was never anything quite as comforting as your own bed. He was simply worn-out. But I was in the same situation.

Now that the house was locked up and secure, our fur-baby was taken care of for the night, and my husband was back where he belonged, I was suddenly exhausted and ready to join Dalton in bed. I pulled off my shirt and tossed it on the end of the bed before I climbed in beside Dalton and pulled up the covers. After reaching over and turning off the light, I scooted just a little closer, and when I could feel Dalton's body heat, I snuggled in and closed my eyes. I was asleep in no time.

Dalton — 24

I was so comfortable I didn't want to get up and move, but the whining in my ear told me that the baby needed to go out. I cracked open my eyes and saw that it was just barely light in the room, and that was because Collin had the curtains open. My husband was right beside me sound asleep. Damn, he was completely worn-out after the past two weeks.

I looked to my right, and sure enough, there was Daisy, whining at me. "All right, girl, let's go," I told her, and she took off out the door. She needed to realize I still couldn't move as fast as she did. Collin's arm snaked out and clamped down across my stomach when I started to roll out of bed.

"Where do you think you're going?" His sleepy voice broke the silence in the room.

"Our daughter needs to go out."

"Then I'll let her out. You go to the bathroom, and then back in bed with you," Collin said before he let me go and then rolled out of bed himself. No fair—he had on sweats, and I didn't get a look at his naked body. He was gone before I could say anything, and I decided to take care of my own morning needs before he returned, like he suggested. Once my bladder was empty and my teeth were brushed, I pulled on a pair of flannel pants and crawled back in bed to relax.

"Now that's exactly what I wanted to see." My gaze flew to the doorway, and I watched as Collin approached with two steaming mugs of coffee. He placed them both down on the nightstand on my side of the bed, and then he sat on the edge of the bed beside me.

"What is it that you wanted to see?" I asked.

"You, in bed, relaxing like you're supposed to be doing."

"Mmm, well, I really hope you're up for rewarding me for doing so this morning. I seem to remember that I was supposed to get some personal attention last night."

"You're a mess, you know that? You would have, except you were asleep by the time I was finished brushing my teeth. Good morning, asshole."

"Good morning, Backstreet." Collin leaned over me and gave me a lingering kiss but quickly pulled away.

"No fair. You've already brushed your teeth."

"Yeah, but you made coffee. What time is it anyway?"

"Early enough that we don't have to rush through a morning blow job," Collin said as he trailed kisses down my chest. I moaned when he got to my nipple and gave it a slight tug with his lips. "Scoot over into the center of the bed. But remember, you promised you'd just lie there and not move much. The doctor was very specific when he said no strenuous activities yet."

I obliged and carefully scooted to the center of our king-sized bed as instructed. Granted, I didn't remember much of the last two weeks, but I knew I always wanted my husband, any way I could get him, and I was curious to see what he had in mind for this morning, other than the mentioned blow job, that is.

"You comfortable? You need pillows rearranged or anything?"

"Nope, I'm good," I replied and watched as Collin pushed off his sweats and then crawled onto the bed. When he yanked my pants off, I didn't protest one bit. My cock was already willing, but with Collin, when wasn't that the case? My husband did it for me. He made me feel things I'd never felt before, and that had me more than happy that he was already my forever.

"I missed you," Collin said as he ran his nose up the length of my shaft. When he got to the head, he stuck out his tongue and gently tickled the exact spot where the head met the shaft. I tried my best to not wiggle, but he knew I was super sensitive there.

"Baby, if you want me to not move around a lot, you need to stop tickling me."

"Mmm, you're probably right. So maybe I should do this instead," Collin said before he grabbed the base of my cock and pulled it upward and then swallowed it down to the root. I moaned and couldn't help but lift my hips slightly while pressing my head back into the pillow and closing my eyes.

"Yesss. Just like that."

"Mmmhmm," Collin replied with my cock deep in his mouth, and the vibrations had my toes curling and my hips lifting again. His hands on my stomach kept me in place, and I just lay there, enjoying the attentions of my husband.

"Baby, I'm not going to last," I warned him as his head continued to bob up and down and he sucked harder. A wet finger probing at my entrance was all it took to send me over the edge and have me filling Collin's mouth with my release. Collin moaned loudly and groaned just as loud as he could, the vibrations too much for my overly sensitive dick, so I gently pushed on Collin's shoulder. When he released my cock, he looked up at me and smiled.

"Feel better?"

"So much better. But now it's my turn."

"No. You have to lie there, remember?" Collin said as he gave my cock one last squeeze and licked up the last drops of my release before he knee-walked up beside me, his hand on his own cock, stroking it at a pace that let me know he was ready to come. "Open up," he said, and just as I did, he pushed his cock into my mouth and groaned. One suck was all it took and Collin was moaning through his orgasm while I tried to keep up and swallow it all.

"Fuck, Dalton," Collin moaned as I grabbed his dick and stroked it through his orgasm. Like him, I wanted every last drop I could get. When he pulled out of my mouth, I wanted to protest but didn't when he scooted down and carefully lay down next to me, his head on my left shoulder.

"I really needed that, baby. Thank you," I told him as I ran my fingers through his hair and then up and down his spine. When he wiggled and tried to move away from my touch, I knew I was successful in tickling him.

"Asshole. Stop, that tickles."

"Yeah, but I'm your asshole, and it's bringing you closer to me, so why would I stop?"

"I don't want to hurt you."

"I appreciate that. But I'm fine. A little sore, but I'm not going to break, okay?"

I felt Collin nod, so I wrapped my arms around him and gave him a tight squeeze. There was a little pulling on my right side, but it was worth it. I needed to reassure my husband, and hopefully, I was well on my way to doing that.

"What time do we need to be at the courthouse?" I asked. I was out of the hospital, and there was no way I wasn't going to be at the preliminary hearing for Carter. He had no idea if Collin and I were alive or dead, and I couldn't wait to see the look on his face when we walked into the courthouse, hand in hand.

"Dalton, you promised you'd behave."

"I am behaving. Now, when?"

"Jacob said nine."

"Okay. We'll need to leave by eight thirty at the latest. That gives us an hour. I don't know about you, but I definitely need that coffee and maybe a shower. After the orgasm you just gave me, I'm ready to go back to sleep."

"You should take a nap, then. You know the doctor said the more rest you get, the faster you'll get back to work."

"Baby, I'm going to be out of work for another four weeks, minimum. Jacob has already said so. I'll have plenty of time to rest and relax. But I'm not going back to bed this morning. You just don't want me to go to court, and that's not happening. I don't have a choice, baby. I'm a key witness; I have to be there."

"You're not a witness; you're his victim," Collin retorted.

"That may be true, but I have to go, nonetheless. Now, are you going to join me in the shower or not?"

"You know I am." Collin got up off the bed and walked to the bathroom. I heard the shower turn on and then the sink. Yeah, he was probably brushing his teeth, something I should do again, considering. I rolled over to the edge of the bed and climbed off and joined my husband in the bathroom to get ready for our day.

"You never told me you were going in uniform," Collin said as he glared at me while I strapped on my new vest over my T-shirt. We'd showered and dried off, and now were getting dressed to head out to the courthouse. Collin, though, wasn't overly amused when I pulled out a clean uniform from the closet.

"Does it matter if I'm in uniform or not?"

"Yes. You're on paid leave. That means you're not supposed to be working."

"True. I am. But I'm also going to the courthouse today in uniform. If I go in uniform, I get to wear my vest as well as my sidearm. Now, do you still have objections?"

Collin stared at me and started to say something several times but in the end opted not to. I raised an eyebrow at him, but he simply turned around and went into the closet and grabbed my boots for me.

"Thank you, baby. I could have gotten them though."

"I realize that. I was just helping."

"And I appreciate it. It'll be okay, you know. We're just going to go and see what the judge has to say and see how things go, all right?" I said as I sat down to pull on my boots. I needed to take a pain pill before we left and grab a quick bite to eat, but otherwise, I was ready to go face Collin's ex. He needed to know he hadn't won.

When we entered the courtroom, I placed my hand on Collin's back and ushered him to the front. He was going between me and Jacob, period. Gavin was on the other side of Jacob, and we all had a direct view of where Carter would be. There was no way he could miss us.

"You okay, baby? You're shaking a little."

"I'm okay, but damn, this man tried to have us killed. And you were shot. I'm a little shaky, I guess."

"It's understandable. If you need to leave we can."

"No, I'm good. I'm here with you, I'm good. I want to see the look on his face when he realizes that we're both still alive."

I nodded at my gorgeous husband and had to agree with his way of thinking. I too could hardly wait to see Carter's face when he was brought in before the judge. Thankfully, we didn't have long to wait. And I must say, orange wasn't his best color. When he spotted us, his eyes got huge, and he kept trying to talk to his lawyer, who kept shushing him.

"Mr. Brown, are you ready to present your charges?"

"Yes, Your Honor."

"Proceed."

"No! You're supposed to be dead! He was supposed to take you out so I could have him!"

"Order! Order! Mr. Dempsey, if you can't control your client, he'll be removed from the courtroom."

Not only was it incredibly difficult to not outright laugh because Carter had just blown his mentally incapacitated plea, but it was hilarious to watch his lawyer try to calm him down. I was on edge, as were Jacob and Gavin.

"Your Honor, at this time, I'd like to ask that I be removed from counsel due to ethical reasons."

"File the paperwork with the clerk, and we'll go from there. Mr. Beaumont, due to your recent outburst, I find you fit for trial and am setting bail at five million dollars. Trial will begin April twenty-second. Bailiff, remove the defendant. Court adjourned."

I finally let a sinister smile grace my face as I wrapped my arm around Collin's shoulders while a cuffed and shackled Carter was walked past us. And just to poke a stick at the man, I even did a little finger wave to him. He made a lurch for us but quickly found himself staring at not only my drawn weapon, but Jacob's and Gavin's as well.

"Try it. I'm within my rights to do it. You've already tried to have me killed. Stay away from what's mine." He was shouting and screaming as the bailiff dragged him from the courtroom. Jacob, Gavin, and I all holstered our sidearms, and when I turned to Collin, I was a little surprised at what I saw. I leaned in and whispered in his ear.

"Just keep that thought until we get home, baby." I gave his ear a gentle nip and then pulled away. Once we were through discussing the upcoming trial and I was finally able to get Collin out of the courthouse building, we were on our way back to the truck when I was struck with an idea.

"Baby?"

"Hmm?" Collin turned and looked at me.

"I just realized something."

"What?"

"Well, we've been married for a little over a month now, and the threat that was Carter and the hit he put out on you is now gone, right?"

"I sure hope so. Dalton, it's fucking cold out here—can we maybe talk in the truck? Preferably with it running and the heat on?"

"Oh, yeah, sure." I grabbed Collin's hand and pulled him behind me, quickly making my way to the truck, which he unlocked as we walked up. I opened the passenger door, and he helped me up into the cab because I wasn't going to make that mistake again. No. Pulling myself up into the truck pulled on my wound, which caused me to yelp and gasp in pain. I was okay with my husband helping. Once the door was shut, he made his way to the driver's side and quickly climbed in and started the engine.

"Now, what did you just realize?"

"That we're married, but really, we never had a honeymoon. I'm off work for the next several weeks, and I know you're dying to get back to work, but I'd really love to take you away for a week. What do you say?"

"I say I know the perfect place," Collin told me before he put the truck in drive and headed back home to Sulfur Springs.

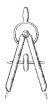

Collin — 25

I was a hundred percent certain that when Dalton told me he wanted to take me on a real honeymoon, he didn't have going to visit my family in California in mind. Actually, I knew that wasn't the case.

"Really, Backstreet? You want to visit your family for our honeymoon?" Dalton asked as we debarked the plane and walked down the jetway.

"Actually, no. But I didn't want to go on a honeymoon while my husband was recovering from a gunshot wound either, but you insisted. I only have a week more I could ask off, and even then, that was pushing it. Once I work the next three hundred days straight, maybe I can ask for time off and we can take a real honeymoon. Like somewhere tropical. That requires very little clothing. Or none at all."

"Why aren't we there?" Dalton asked, stopping in the middle of the airport. Other passengers walked around us, some smiling, some glaring.

"Because you still haven't been cleared to have sex, and I plan on sexing it up with you when we actually do go on our honeymoon, so start saving, asshole. We're going someplace like Tahiti or Bora Bora or something."

"Backstreet, you do realize they're both in French Polynesia, right? They're almost right next to each other. And have you ever *looked* at the accounts?"

"Yeah, I knew they were close. But it was just an example. And why would I look at the accounts? We combined them last month when we got married. I know what I make, and I don't spend much."

"I'm not exactly poor. And neither are you. I've made decent money for years and have had nothing to spend it on. If you want to go to Tahiti or Bora Bora, then let's go buy tickets. We already have our passports. And to hell with what the doctor said. You know very well I'm able to do just about anything you've asked me to do. I thought I proved that last night?"

I stared at the man in front of me that I had married. He had very valid points. But I only had another week I could take off without feeling even more guilty. Sean and Jasper were amazing and understood, but still. Could we? Really? I looked at Dalton's pleading blue eyes and melted on the spot.

"Shit. Let's get our bag and see if we can get reservations last minute. It's February for shit's sake; everyone wants to go to

Tahiti or somewhere warm right about now. I'll never forgive myself if you get hurt while we're there though, so don't overdo it, all right?"

"Baby, you know I'll be good. But trust me on this one. I want to treat you to a real honeymoon. Especially since I stole a real wedding from you."

"What are you talking about? Our wedding was perfect. We're married, aren't we?"

"Yes."

"And just because we didn't spend a small fortune and wear uncomfortable penguin suits, that doesn't mean we aren't any more married than someone that did those things, right?"

"Again, yes."

"Dalton, I love you, but I married *you*. Not a wedding."

"Love you, too. Now, grab our bag before it goes around the conveyer and we have to wait for it to come back around," Dalton told me as I looked over my shoulder and reached for our bag as it moved past me. We'd both packed incredibly light and were sharing a checked bag. Hopefully, what we had would be useful in our final destination. "Let's see, which do you prefer? Tahiti or Bora Bora? To get to Bora Bora, we have to first fly into Tahiti, and then take a float plane to Bora Bora. It's a little more exotic it seems, so I'm voting for that," Dalton said as he looked at his phone.

"Should you really be spending thirteen hours on a plane? I mean, you did okay on the flight out here, but it was short. What about thirteen hours? How are your lungs doing?"

"Baby, if you don't want to go now, then let's rent a car and drive up the coast or something. But I'm begging you, can we please not spend our honeymoon with your family?"

"It's so unfair. Are you sure you're okay?"

"Positive. Which is it? Flight or car and up the coast? Or down the coast—it's warmer down."

"Flight. I want you to relax. And you're not going to unless we're away from everything."

"It's like you know me or something, baby. There, flights, car, and hotel booked. We need to head to check-in. Our flight leaves in four hours."

I couldn't believe it. I was actually running off to Tahiti with Dalton. Was this real? I pulled out my phone and gave Daniel a quick text and let him know our change in plans. I showed Dalton the pissed-off responses and then turned my phone off. He did the same and smiled at me.

"You ready to go stand in line?"

"Yes. So ready," I replied with a huge smile on my face. This was completely unlike me, but I was with Dalton, and I was ready for this. We made our way to the front check-in desks, checked our bag, got our boarding passes, and then went back through security.

All in all, not how I planned on spending the day, but it was going to be worth it.

"Food. We need food," I told Dalton as I yanked on his hand and pulled him toward a restaurant. I was hungry, and he was going to need to eat because he was due for more pain meds.

"A late lunch sounds good." Dalton said as we entered the restaurant. After stuffing ourselves with thick, juicy bacon cheeseburgers and fries, we paid our bill and went to our gate to wait for our flight.

"Baby?"

"Hmm?" I asked, looking up at my husband.

"Isn't that your brother?"

"What?" I yelled just a little too loudly. No way. Please. No way. I slowly turned my head the direction Dalton was indicating and just about died when I saw a pissed-off Daniel storming up to us. No fucking way.

"Hey, Danny boy. What's shakin'?" Dalton asked once my brother was in front of us. It took every ounce of willpower to not bust out laughing at that. Daniel hated being called anything but…well…Daniel.

"What are you two doing? You can't go flying off somewhere else."

"Why not?" I asked. If there was a reason, maybe we should reconsider.

"I was hoping we could spend some time together now that things seemed to have calmed down."

"Wait, you're telling me you bought a plane ticket to get through security so you could complain that you're not going to get to chat with your brother?"

"Dalton, behave."

"No, baby. We're on our honeymoon. You don't spend your honeymoon with family. Period. You spend it fucking like rabbits, taking long walks on the beach, and eating too much high-fat food that we'll regret next week when we're back in Wyoming freezing our asses off."

"Wait. You're on your honeymoon? You said you two were coming for a visit."

"Yeah, well, then when we got here, Dalton decided we'd take a last-minute honeymoon and booked a package to Tahiti."

"Seriously?" Daniel asked, surprised.

"Yes. I wanted to have an actual honeymoon. Without Carter looking over our heads. Your brother deserves it."

"So why are you sitting here talking to me, then?"

"We're waiting on our flight. It doesn't leave for another hour," I told my brother. "Besides, why are you here? And how did you get back here?"

"I told you why, but that was before I knew your hubby was taking you honeymooning. And I have this badge that gets me through security since Stealth's plane is stationed out of here."

"Yeah, how does that work, exactly?"

I groaned at Dalton's question. Daniel would be here for hours talking about his job. I was ready for a vacation.

"Some other time, Dalton. You two have fun. And go fuck like bunnies, like you said," Daniel told us as he winked at Dalton and leaned down to give me a hug.

"That's it? You came all this way for that?"

"No, I came all this way because you said you were coming for a visit, and then you changed your mind. You never said you were on your honeymoon. Go fuck. Have fun. But remember, use sunblock. A sunburned dick is painful."

When a pair of older, mature ladies gasped, Dalton and I laughed hard, until Dalton gasped in pain.

"Oh shit, I needed that. Thanks, Daniel."

"Anytime. Remember, lube and sand don't mix. See you two in a few weeks!" Daniel said over his shoulder as he walked off. The old ladies glared at us, and I was tempted to give it to them. Instead, I leaned in and pulled Dalton's mouth to mine and moaned when he slipped his tongue into my mouth. Yeah, this was how I wanted to start my honeymoon. This was what I'd been waiting for. This happy, carefree, there's only us feeling. It'd been missing for quite some time.

"Baby?"

"Hmm?"

"What did your brother mean when he said he'd see us in a couple weeks?"

"I'm not sure. Shit. You don't think they're coming to Wyoming for a visit again, do you? I mean, I love my family and all, but I'm getting a little tired of having to share our space. I want to christen each and every room in the house. We haven't done that yet."

"Well, hopefully they'll stay at one of the lodges or something."

Our flight started boarding, and then we were finally, at last, on our way. I'd never been and was looking forward to spending the next six days and six nights in Tahiti with Dalton.

"Hey, are we staying in Tahiti, or are we going over to Bora Bora?" I asked, midflight.

"I booked us a bungalow over the water in Bora Bora. That good?"

"Perfect." I snuggled up with Dalton and dozed off during the long flight. Almost fourteen hours later, we were touching down in what was only a speck in the middle of a big blue ocean.

"Oh my. Wow, Dalton look at this place." I said as we taxied on the runway. We still had a little farther to go, with another short flight scheduled. "You know, this sounded so much better before we left. It's been a long flight. How you doing, baby?"

"I hurt. And I'm ready to lie down and just sleep."

Ninety minutes later, we were checked in to our bungalow, and Dalton was doing just that. I felt so bad, so guilty for coming now. The flight was hard on him, and I'd figured it would be, but he wanted to give me a honeymoon. I stripped off my clothes and showered in the too-small shower, and once I was dried off, I joined my husband in sleep-time slumber. He'd taken the first shower and then promptly passed out. I needed to take better care of my husband. Who knew how many days it'd take him to recover.

I woke up to the sun shining directly in my eyes and Dalton still sound asleep beside me. I got up and closed the window and curtains, and after relieving my bladder, I went out and closed all of the other windows as well. The clock on the wall said it was just after six, so I assumed that meant just after six in the morning. We needed to get on a schedule, but first, more sleep. The next time I woke up, it was to Dalton nibbling on my neck.

"Mmm, there you are. Good morning, hubby."

"Mmm, good morning. Is it still morning? It was sixish earlier when I got up and closed the curtains."

"Yeah, but just barely. I'm starving and ordered room service. It'll be here anytime now, so you might want to put on some shorts or something."

"Really? You wake me by nibbling on my neck, getting me all excited, and then tell me to get dressed. Really?"

"I'm sorry, baby. I'm really hungry. It's been a day since either of us have eaten anything substantial. I need to take my meds, and you know how it is."

"Shit. I'm sorry. Let me get dressed. Why didn't you wake me?"

"I just did."

"Yeah, but why didn't you wake me earlier?"

"I've been up all of ten minutes. Long enough to use the bathroom and call in for food."

"And it's going to be ready that fast?"

"I think I ordered stuff they have ready-made or something, I don't know. They said ten minutes."

As I pulled my shorts up my legs, there was a knock on the door. Dalton got up to go answer it and let the young lady in. She had a beautiful smile and was directing it at my husband. *Yeah, you're barking up the wrong tree, lady. He doesn't bat for your team.*

"What did you order?" I asked, walking over to where she was dropping off the tray. She glanced at me and then Dalton and back at me again. I wrapped my arms around his bare torso and kissed the angry-looking scars on his back.

"I ordered breakfast. I figured we'd go out and explore and find something for lunch in a couple hours," Dalton said, lacing our fingers together. He signed the ticket, thanked the young woman, and walked her to the door, all with me glued to his back.

"Possessive much?"

"Damn right. You're mine. Now, let's eat. You said you were hungry. Sit and I'll get your meds, and we'll eat and then go explore."

And eat we did. And explore. And make love. We spent the majority of our time in the bungalow because Dalton still tired easily, and we needed to allow him to rest. But he didn't complain when I lubed up his cock, crawled on top of him, and gently rode him until we were both moaning and groaning through our orgasms. The only real complaint he had was that I was too gentle, and he still had some pain when I tried to top him. I was perfectly content to be the bottom for as long as needed. Sure, we loved to take turns, and we would go back to that once Dalton was fully healed. But for now, he was the one who was getting ridden. Not that he complained, too much.

Unfortunately, our time in Bora Bora came to an end all too soon. We were returning to the frigidly cold temperatures and snow in Wyoming, and it was quite a shock.

"I've missed Daisy. Can we swing by and pick her up before we go home?"

"Dalton, Crooked Bend is out of the way from here," I said while laughing.

"I know, but I miss our girl."

"We can swing by and get her. Are you sure you're okay to do so? I can drop you off at home if you want and then go over and get her."

"No. I want to go."

"All right, we'll go together." I drove to Crooked Bend, taking a chance and going straight to the station since I figured Gavin would be working. I figured correctly. Daisy whined and cried like she hadn't seen Dalton in forever, but I rolled my eyes at Gavin, who just smiled. We thanked him for watching her for us, and then were on our way home, finally.

Epilogue
Dalton

I was a lucky asshole, and I knew it. I watched Collin as he played with Daisy out in the snow. We'd finally retrieved Knight and had inquired about purchasing another mount for Collin to ride. Isaac and Simon were only too happy to help with that. I had to laugh at them, but I also knew that any mount we got from them would be top-of-the-line, and I could feel good about the beautiful man in front of me on it.

"Hey, you two about ready to go inside? I don't know about you, but I'm getting cold," I shouted at the pair. I loved that Daisy loved Collin as much as I did and vice versa. We had our rough patches, and we still didn't agree on everything, but it didn't matter. What mattered was that we were together, and we were happy and in love.

Collin joined me, his blue eyes dancing with happiness, his cheeks rosy red from the cold, and his smile just for me. When his lips met mine, they were cold, as expected, and I couldn't wait to go inside and warm him up.

"Mmm, as much as I love kissing you, I thought you said you were getting cold?"

"I am. Come on, let's get you inside and get you warmed up," I told him as I laced my fingers with his and tugged him into the house with me. Daisy happily followed. After getting her normal toweling off, she went to the water bowl, drank half, and then plopped down in front of the fireplace for a nap.

"She has the right idea, you know."

"She does? What's that? A nap? Are you saying you want to go take a nap, Backstreet?"

"Yes and no. I'm always up for going to bed with you, but I'm not really sleepy, so I was hoping that maybe you'd be able to help me with that?"

I turned and looked at my husband. He had that look in his eyes that said he was ready for me to do incredibly wicked things to him.

"Oh, it's like that, is it? Then why are you still down here, and why are you still dressed? Upstairs with ya!" I couldn't help but smile as Collin laughed and took off toward the stairs. I checked the doors to make sure they were locked, and then I followed my husband, albeit at a slower pace. I was still getting there, but I was better. It was the middle of March, and it had been six weeks since I'd been shot, and the only time I really hurt was when I spent too long outside in the super cold temps, or if I tried to lift something too heavy.

Collin was a trooper, and even though he'd kill me if I ever told him, he was worth it, and I'd do it all over again if it meant he was safe. I'd made a commitment to him, and I meant it.

I found him in the bedroom, unlacing his boots and struggling with the frozen laces. "Need some help there?"

"Maybe? I'm not going to complain if you want to help. My fingers are cold, and that's not helping."

I held out my hand, and Collin place his boot on my thigh. I untied the first one easily enough and then the other boot. I sat down beside him and pulled off my own boots, then quickly stripped out of my clothes and walked into the bathroom to turn on the shower.

"Are we showering first? We usually need a shower after."

"True, but you're cold, and I want to warm you up before I get you all dirty. Besides, who says we can't have fun in the shower?" I asked as I pulled my husband into the oversized shower with me. That was definitely something I'd missed while we were on our honeymoon. We'd agreed we wanted to take a trip every year and do something fun. There were so many places we could travel to and see, and it was something I was looking forward to doing with Collin.

"Hey, where'd you go?"

"Sorry, was just thinking, I know we have almost a year, but I was thinking about next year's trip."

"Oh yeah?" Collin asked before he ducked his head under the warm water. It must have felt good because he moaned and rubbed his fingers through his hair. "The showerhead feels heavenly. Let's always keep this one."

I chuckled at that, but he had a point. It did feel good. "Unless they come up with one that's better, we'll keep that one. Deal." I poured shampoo into my hand and then lathered his short blond hair. While he rinsed, I lathered up the loofah and then washed the rest of his body. I quickly washed, and then we traded places so I could wash my hair. Only Collin had other ideas, and I felt his hands start roaming over my naked, wet flesh.

"Mmm, that feels amazing, baby."

"Good. It's supposed to. Turn around after you rinse your hair."

I quickly rinsed the shampoo out of my hair and then did as instructed and turned my back toward Collin and faced the tile wall.

"All right, Deputy, spread 'em," Collin said while laughing. I couldn't help it; I joined him, but I was certainly up for playing his little game. We'd had a lot of fun with my handcuffs as well as my uniform and even some of his ties. But I loved it when he took control and made my body sing.

I felt Collin spread my cheeks, and then the warmth of his mouth and tongue were on my opening, and I couldn't keep quiet. Besides, Daisy didn't care how loud we were. Something I was thankful for. I reached down and started stroking my throbbing cock to the same rhythm as Collin's tongue probing me, but he was gone before I could get far.

"Hey, why'd you…" I stopped midsentence when I felt a very slick finger probing at my entrance. "Yesss, please, Collin. I need you so much."

"I know, baby. It's been too long since I've been inside you, and I promise, as long as you don't yelp, I'm going to pound your ass as hard as I can," Collin whispered next to my ear before he bit down on my neck, causing me to moan louder.

"Collin, please."

"Is this what you want, baby?" Collin asked as I felt his cock replace his fingers. When I nodded and braced my palms against the wall in front of me, I felt Collin slide into my channel in one smooth, slow push.

"Yesss, more, I'm good," I begged. I needed this so much.

"Yeah, you might be good, but I'm struggling here. It's been a while since I've been inside you, and I'm about to blow."

"Shit. Just blow and keep going. It's not going to take me long either. Promise."

"But I wanted more for your first time after the doctor cleared you," Collin told me as he slowly moved in and out of me.

"Baby, anything with you is heaven. Hard or slow, it doesn't matter, I'm not going to last long," I told him while panting. He felt too good, and already, he'd found my prostate and was pegging it with each and every thrust.

Collin wrapped his arms under mine, grabbed the front of my shoulders, and let me have what I so desperately wanted. We were both shouting our release within moments, him inside me and me on the tiles. He leaned his forehead on my shoulder, and I just stood there, willing my shaky legs to not give out.

"Let's get you cleaned up again. I promise, I'll make it better for you next time."

"Baby, there was nothing wrong with this time. Any chance I get to spend with you is a good thing," I told him as we cleaned up and got out. "Besides, we have our whole entire lives ahead of us to make love. But sometimes, quick is just as good as long and sweet. You know why?"

"Why?" Collin asked.

"Because I love you," I said as I pulled my very naked husband into my arms.

"I love you, too."

"Good, because you're stuck with me. Now, get in bed. I've gotta outdo you," I said as I gave his ass a slap.

"Asshole."

"Yeah, but I'm your asshole and you love me."

"Yeah, I really do," Collin said as he climbed into our king-sized bed. Damn, I sure loved my husband.

About the Author

Thank you so much for reading Protecting My Commitment. Up next in the series is Hawke and Trace!

Hugs,
Taylor

Want to know when my next book is being released? How about giveaways and sales?

You can find me on Facebook here:
https://www.facebook.com/TaylorRylan
My reader group is here:
https://www.facebook.com/groups/TaylorsTroublemakers/
You can find me on Instagram here:
https://www.instagram.com/author_taylor_rylan/
You can find me on Twitter here:
https://twitter.com/TaylorRylan1
Book Bub here:
https://www.bookbub.com/profile/taylor-rylan
You can visit my web page here:
www.taylorrylan.com
Join my newsletter here:
bit.ly/TaylorRylanNews

I promise not to spam you or ever sell your email address to anyone. My newsletter will be uscd solely for marketing and announcements about upcoming releases and sales.
Feel free to contact me! I would love to hear from you.
Thank you!

Also by Taylor Rylan

Contemporary Series
Men of Crooked Bend Series

My Forever, My Always: Men of Crooked Bend Book 1
https://mybook.to/MFMAebook
My Choice, My Chance: Men of Crooked Bend Book 2
https://mybook.to/MCMCebook
My Survivor, My Savior: Men of Crooked Bend Book 3
https://mybook.to/MSMSebook
My Truth, My Future: Men of Crooked Bend Book 4
https://mybook.to/MTMFebook
My Love, My Valentine: Men of Crooked Bend Book 5
https://mybook.to/MLMVebook
My Heart, My Home: Men of Crooked Bend Book 6
https://mybook.to/MHMHebook
My Christmas, My Crooked Bend: Men of Crooked Bend Book 7
https://mybook.to/MCMCBebook
Logan's Loves: Men of Crooked Bend Book 8
https://mybook.to/LogansLoves
Jacob's Joy: Men of Crooked Bend Book 9
https://mybook.to/JacobsJoy
Simon's Surprise: Men of Crooked Bend Book 10
https://mybook.to/SimonsSurprise

Sulfur Springs Series

Protecting My Commitment: Sulfur Springs Book 1
https://mybook.to/PMCebook
Rescuing My Angel: Sulfur Springs Book 2
https://mybook.to/RMAebook
Saving My Sanity: Sulfur Springs Book 3
https://mybook.to/SMSebook
Surrendering My Affection: Sulfur Springs Book 4
https://mybook.to/SMAebook
Our Valentine Surprise
https://mybook.to/OVSebook
Disarming My Destiny: Sulfur Springs Book 5
https://mybook.to/DMDebook
Healing My Amor: Sulfur Springs Book 6
https://mybook.to/HMAebook
Wrangling My Heart: Sulfur Springs Book 7
https://mybook.to/WMHebook

Contemporary Standalones

Sixteen Weeks
https://mybook.to/SixteenWeeks

Shifters/MPREG
Honey Creek Den Series

War's Mate: Honey Creek Den Book 1
https://mybook.to/WarsMate
Troy's Warlock: Honey Creek Den Book 2
https://mybook.to/TroysWarlock
Ryker's Enchantment: Honey Creek Den Book 3
https://mybook.to/RykersEnchantment
Grayson's Enlightenment: Honey Creek Den Book 4
https://mybook.to/GraysonsEnlightenment
Gage's Serenity: Honey Creek Den Book 5
https://mybook.to/GagesSerenity
Jules's Sanctuary: Honey Creek Den Book 6
https://mybook.to/JulesSanctuary

Timber Valley Wolf Pack Series

Forest's Hope: Timber Valley Wolf Pack Book 1
https://mybook.to/ForestsHope
Sterling's Treasure: Timber Valley Wolf Pack Book 2
https://mybook.to/SterlingsTreasure
Alistair's One: Timber Valley Wolf Pack Book 3
https://mybook.to/AlistairsOne

Printed in Great Britain
by Amazon